Catch the Wind
My Journey with Caroline

by Kathleen Ernst

⭐ American Girl®

Published by American Girl Publishing
Copyright © 2014 American Girl

Questions or comments? Call 1-800-845-0005,
visit **americangirl.com**, or write to Customer Service,
American Girl, 8400 Fairway Place, Middleton, WI 53562.

Printed in China
14 15 16 17 18 19 20 LEO 10 9 8 7 6 5 4 3 2 1

All American Girl marks, Beforever™, Caroline™, and
Caroline Abbott™ are trademarks of American Girl.

Cover image by Michael Dwornik and Juliana Kolesova

Cataloging-in-Publication Data available from the Library of Congress

*For the readers in Sackets Harbor,
with thanks for giving Caroline—and me—
such a warm welcome*

Beforever

Beforever is about making connections.
It's about exploring the past, finding your
place in the present, and thinking about the
possibilities your future can bring. And it's about
seeing the common thread that ties girls from
all times together. The inspiring characters you
will meet stand up for what they care about
most: Helping others. Protecting the earth.
Overcoming injustice. Through their courageous
stories, discover how staying true to your own
beliefs will help make your world better
today—and tomorrow.

A Journey Begins

This book is about Caroline, but it's also about a girl like you who travels back in time to Caroline's world of 1812. You, the reader, get to decide what happens in the story. The choices you make will lead to different journeys and new discoveries.

When you reach a page in this book that asks you to make a decision, choose carefully. The decisions you make will lead to different endings. (Hint: Use a pencil to check off your choices. That way, you'll never read the same story twice.)

Want to try another ending? Read the book again—and then again. Find out what happens to you and Caroline when you make different choices.

Before your journey ends, take a peek into the past, on page 190, to discover more about Caroline's time.

School is out, and since summer is my absolutely
favorite season, I should be having a great morning. Dad made chocolate-chip pancakes for breakfast.
Mom said I don't have to take swimming lessons this
summer, which is good news since swimming is my
absolutely least favorite activity.

But my five-year-old twin sisters, Britney and Sasha,
just hauled a photo album into the kitchen. I had fun
helping them make it last summer, right after we all
went camping up north, but I don't want to see it now.
We won't have a family camping trip this year. Mom,
who recently joined the U.S. Navy, is about to leave on
her ship for eight whole months.

Sasha heaves the album onto the table. Mom smiles
when the book flops open to a picture of our family
taken the morning after a thunderstorm. We'd hardly
gotten any sleep, and everything was muddy, but
for some reason once the sun came up we all started
laughing.

Dad comes over to see, and he smiles too. "Oh, that
was an adventure," he says.

Britney turns a page and accidentally shoves the
album farther across the table. "Don't get maple syrup

on the album," Mom tells her. Then she looks at me. "Will you please put the plates in the dishwasher?"

All the sadness and worry and disappointment I've been trying to hide for weeks comes boiling out. "I don't want to put the plates in the dishwasher!" I shout.

The twins' little-kid eyes open really wide. Mom's eyes scrunch up, though. She always looks like that when she's unhappy with me.

Normally when I see that look I quit whatever I'm doing. Not today. "And I don't want you to go away!" I add. "I wish you'd never joined the navy!"

"Hey!" Dad says sharply. "Apologize to your mother. Right *now*."

My throat starts to swell. My eyes fill with tears. As if what Mom's doing isn't bad enough, now Dad is mad at me.

That's just *it*. I turn and run outside, slamming the door behind me.

Now that I've left the air-conditioning, the air slaps my skin like a hot, damp towel. I run across the lawn and plunge down the path that leads through the woods to the pond.

This has always been my special place. It's shady here, and quiet. I plop down on the grassy bank, bring my knees up, bury my face in my arms, and cry.

I haven't cried this hard since I was little. As little as the twins, maybe. Thinking of them makes me angry all over again. I haven't heard Mom tell *them* that they have to do extra chores while she's gone. I haven't heard Dad tell *them* that they have to be extra brave. I'm tired of being the oldest! It's not fair.

❀ *Turn to page 4.*

A fter a while I run out of tears. I raise my head and wipe my eyes. My breath is all shuddery and my nose is running.

"Would you like a tissue?" Mom asks quietly. I hadn't heard her following me, but now she sits down on the bank too.

I wipe my eyes and blow my nose. I'm really afraid that Mom is going to start scolding me. Instead she sighs. "I'm sorry this is so hard on you," she says.

"*Ple-e-e-ease* don't go away," I beg. "I want you to stay home with us!"

Mom's mouth twists sideways like it does when she's thinking. Finally she says, "Sometimes it helps to talk things through. Can you tell me exactly what you're afraid of?"

I've never told Mom that I'm afraid, but she's smart about guessing stuff. I'm bursting to say, *"Everything!"* I have to clench my teeth to hold that word inside.

It's true, though. I'm afraid that I won't have time to do *anything* except help Dad with the twins while Mom's gone. After all, Dad has his own job as a hospital nurse. I won't have any time to spend with my friends.

Even worse, I'm afraid I'll miss Mom so much that I'll be miserable every single second of every single day. I'm afraid that Mom will get hurt. That would be bad any time, but extra-bad if she's far away.

Worst of all is imagining Mom sailing away on the ocean. Those navy ships are huge—but still puny compared to all the water in an ocean. Just thinking about deep water makes my heart thump in my chest.

"Sweetie," Mom says, "the ship I'll be on is designed to help keep everyone on board safe. Would you like to hear more about that?"

"No." I don't want to hear one single thing about the navy ship that's going to take her so far away.

As if she reads my mind, Mom stops talking about the ship. "Dad will be counting on you while I'm away."

"I *know*." I sound kind of grumpy, but I can't help it.

Mom gently brushes my hair away from my forehead. "I don't *want* to be away from my family for so long, you know," she says. "I'll miss you every single minute."

"Really?" I ask.

"Really," Mom says. "But I'm also proud to serve my country, and as a navy doctor, I can help lots of people while we're deployed. My father served in the navy, and his father before him. It's a chain of service that hasn't been broken for over two hundred years! I want to carry on that tradition."

I pick a long stem of grass and wind it around my thumb. Tradition seems like a terrible reason for a mom to leave her kids.

"And I want to make the world a safer place," she adds quietly. "For you and for your sisters. And for the children *you* may have one day."

That's more than I can imagine, so I don't answer.

"I need you to be brave," Mom adds. "Can you try to do that for me?"

I shrug, still not looking at her. Dad already talked to me about that. He said I especially need to be brave on the day Mom leaves. "If you weep and wail, you'll just make it harder on Mom," he said. "We need to tell her that we're proud of her, and that we love her. Then we need to smile and wave good-bye."

Just thinking about watching Mom go away makes tears sting my eyes all over again. In fact, I'm pretty

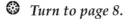

sure that I won't even go with everybody else to see Mom off. Maybe I'll just hide out right here by the pond. Then I wouldn't have to say good-bye at all.

I wish I *were* brave, like Mom. But I'm not.

❀ *Turn to page 8.*

A few minutes pass before Mom says, "I want to give you something." She holds out her hand with fingers curled over the gift.

She's got a present for me? I hadn't expected that, and I feel a teensy bit better. Mom and Dad have promised that I can get my ears pierced on my next birthday. Maybe she picked out special earrings for me!

What she gives me isn't a little jewelry box, though. Instead, my present is something round and hard and made of metal. A piece of glass protects a dial on one side.

I glance at Mom. "Um . . . is it a pocket watch?"

"No," Mom says. "Take a closer look."

There are only a few letters on the dial: N, NE, E, SE, S, SW, W, NW. Now I get it—it's a compass. I used one to navigate on a Girl Scout hike last spring. Our leader taught us that the letters stand for North, Northeast, East, and so on. And I learned that the needle always points north.

"You're giving me a compass?" I ask, totally confused. What's the point in having a compass when you can use GPS to navigate wherever you need to go?

"I'm giving you a very old compass," Mom explains.

"My father gave it to me when he was shipping out for a long voyage at sea. He got it from his father, who got it from his father, and so on. This compass goes back to the very first person in our family to serve in the navy. That was during the War of 1812."

We haven't studied the War of 1812 in school yet, so I don't really know anything about it. I can tell that Mom thinks I should be excited about this, but honestly, I wish a pair of sparkly earrings had gotten passed down in my family instead.

Mom gives me her *This is important* look. "Sailors in our family have always used this compass to navigate."

"Oh," I say. What does that have to do with me?

"I hope it will help remind you to steer a steady course while I'm at sea," Mom says. "And I hope it helps remind you about our family tradition of service to our country."

I don't say anything. All this compass is going to remind me of is Mom choosing to join the navy and go away instead of finding a job where she could stay home with her family.

"This compass means a lot to me," Mom adds, and her voice gets a little shaky. "Over the years it's helped

many people in our family find their way home."

"Then you'd better keep it," I tell her.

Instead of taking it back, Mom closes my fingers over the compass. Then she gets up, kisses the top of my head, and starts walking back to the house.

I stay where I am, relieved that Mom has left me alone. I don't feel like being with my family right now. I don't want to talk about her going away anymore. And I especially don't want anything to do with this compass!

After a moment I lie down and wriggle closer to the edge of the bank. I see my reflection in the still pond water below. My eyes are all red and funny-looking from crying.

I hold out the compass in front of me. The gold part is dull and dented, and the glass is cloudy. What am I supposed to do with it? I'm tempted to throw the compass into the pond, but I don't quite dare.

I turn the compass in my hand, but the needle on the dial keeps pointing in the same direction—north. Right now it's pointed straight at me. The needle looks like a little arrow aimed at my heart. I think about how Mom going away *feels* like an arrow in my heart.

A tiny whirring sound in my right ear distracts me. There's a hummingbird hovering not six inches away! I hold perfectly still. Hummingbirds zip around so fast that it's hard to get a good look at one.

Suddenly movement in the water pulls my attention from the bird. My reflection is trembling, as if someone had tossed a rock into the pond. The water ripples and sloshes until my face becomes a blur. Feeling dizzy, I close my eyes, the compass clutched tight in my hand.

After a moment the dizziness passes. I slowly open my eyes. The water below is still, and I can see my reflection again.

Except . . . it's not me.

I blink. The face in the water is mine, but my hair is covered by an old-fashioned bonnet. This morning I put on a bright red T-shirt with sequins, but now I seem to be wearing something pale blue with white lace around the collar. And instead of the pond's muddy bottom, I see stones through clear sparkling water.

That's so spooky that I scramble to my feet. I almost trip because that pale blue top I saw reflected is actually a long dress. I slap at it, as if that might make it

turn back into my comfy old shorts, but nothing happens. My sandals have turned into black shoes.

Gulping, I take a look around.

The summer heat is familiar, but that's all. Instead of the little pond behind my house, I'm beside a humongous lake that stretches away into the distance.

What is going on? I feel dizzy all over again.

"Are you looking for warships too?"

I whirl around. A blonde girl about my age is walking toward me, easily making her way over the stones. She's wearing a long pink dress and looks as if she belongs in a play or something.

I open my mouth, then close it again. Finally I stammer, "Did—did you say *warships*?"

The girl looks out over the lake and clenches her fists. "They're out there," she says. She looks half angry and half scared. "We drove them off yesterday, but they'll be back."

I do not like the sound of *that*. "Um . . . who, exactly?" I ask.

"The British, of course!" she exclaims. "Those black-hearted British will repair their ships and sail back across Lake Ontario again."

Back to *where*? "This might sound stupid," I say, "but can you tell me where we are, exactly?"

She looks startled. "Why . . . you've reached Sackets Harbor, New York. The village is just around the curve of the bluff." She grins, and suddenly the worry is gone from her face. "My name is Caroline Abbott. Who are you?"

Her smile is so nice that I can't help smiling back, as if we're sure to become friends. I introduce myself. "And I just arrived," I add, to help explain why I have absolutely no idea what's going on.

"So you don't know about yesterday's battle," Caroline says. "British ships formed a line in front of Sackets Harbor and fired cannonballs at us! It lasted for hours."

My jaw drops when she speaks of battle and cannonballs. Have I really and truly landed in the middle of a war? *Oh Mom*, I think, *I wish you'd stayed with me back there by our pond!*

"But our gun crew fired back," Caroline's saying proudly. "And I helped!" Since she's just a kid, I can't imagine how she was able to help a gun crew. Before I can find out she asks, "Have you traveled far?"

That almost makes me laugh, even though it isn't funny. "Yes," I say. "Very, very far."

"Are you traveling by yourself?" She looks behind me, as if expecting someone else to appear.

I look around too. We're standing on a narrow strip of stony shore. A rough rock wall, all drippy with moss and ferns, rises straight up behind us. No one else is in sight. "Yes," I tell her. "I'm alone. And I guess I . . . well, I sort of got lost."

"Now that war has been declared, lots and lots of people are traveling to Sackets Harbor." Caroline sighs. "I think eighteen-twelve is going to be a very difficult year."

Eighteen-twelve? I seem to have traveled over two hundred years back in time!

Caroline looks over the lake again, and her blue-green eyes fill with a sadness so deep that it makes my own heart ache. "My papa is a prisoner of war."

"That's terrible!" I gasp. "I'm truly sorry." I reach out and squeeze Caroline's hand. She squeezes back.

I can't help imagining how I'd feel if something like that happened to Mom one day. And suddenly, it's all just too much. My fingers start to hurt, and I realize

that I'm gripping the compass Mom gave me—

The compass! All this craziness started when the compass needle pointed at my heart. Maybe if I point the compass needle away from my heart, I can get back home!

"Pardon me," I murmur. "I, um . . . I think I dropped something." While she's looking across the water, I hurry behind a rock outcropping. I sidestep until the quivering compass needle points straight away from me. *Please,* I think. *Please, please, please . . .* The dizziness comes, and I close my eyes.

⚙ *Turn to page 16.*

When the dizziness fades, I open my eyes again. I'm lying on the bank of the familiar pond. The hummingbird I saw right before traveling back to 1812 is still whirring in the air right beside me. I blink, and the tiny bird zooms away.

I'm so relieved that I flop back on the grass and start to laugh. I'm home! And clearly no time passed *here* while I was back in 1812, meeting Caroline— a hummingbird wouldn't stay in one spot for long.

Caroline, I think, remembering how friendly she was. When she grinned at me, it felt like I'd known her forever. And in those last few seconds, right before I traveled back home, her eyes were so full of worry and sadness that they made me feel sad *for* her. I know what it feels like to be scared and upset. I wish I'd at least been nice enough to ask Caroline if she was OK. Her father was a prisoner, and I didn't stick around long enough to find out how it happened, or how long he'd been gone.

I sigh, knowing I'll wonder about Caroline forever and ever if I don't go back. And now that I know how this compass-thing works . . .

Still, how smart is it to go back to a time when

cannonballs might start falling any second? My dad is real big on making good choices. Whenever I mess up, he reminds me that I had other options. I'm pretty sure he'd think that going two hundred years back in time—and landing right in the middle of a war— is the worst choice ever.

⚙ *To stay in the present, turn to page 22.*

⚙ *To return to 1812, turn to page 24.*

I take a big breath. "I'll come too," I tell Caroline. I can hardly believe I just agreed to go sailing! But I've already traveled over two hundred years back in time. What's a little trip on Lake Ontario? *You can do this,* I tell myself. *You can. You can.*

"Oh good," Caroline says. She sounds excited, but I also see relief in her eyes. Maybe she feels a teensy bit nervous about heading out with Lieutenant Woolsey too, and having a friend along—even a new friend like me—will make it easier for her. That makes me feel better about my decision.

"Come along, then," Lieutenant Woolsey says impatiently.

Before Caroline and I can follow him, Mrs. Abbott plants herself in front of us and says, "Girls, take heed whenever Lieutenant Woolsey gives you an instruction." She makes a big deal of looking each of us in the eye—just like my own mom does when she wants to be sure I'm listening.

"Yes ma'am," I say.

Then I follow Caroline out the door, hoping like crazy that I haven't made the biggest mistake of my life.

We leave the shipyard, passing tidy brick homes and wooden ones neatly painted white, red, or yellow. But some of the shops near the harbor look like shacks that just got nailed together. The main street is so crowded that it's hard to walk without getting jostled. The air is noisy with shouts, laughter, and the calls of a man peddling vegetables from a wheelbarrow. It all seems a bit messier than what I've seen about olden times on TV. The air smells a little fishy, with the odors of horse poop and stinky tar mixed in. I can't help grabbing my nose when a few men in patched clothes shove past. When Caroline sees me, she puts a hand over her mouth, but I can tell that she's giggling.

When we reach the navy dock, we follow Lieutenant Woolsey into a small rowboat. Another sailor rows us through the harbor to a schooner. It's made of wood and has two really tall masts. It's tricky to climb up a ladder to the deck in my long dress, but I finally make it without falling into the water.

I feel tingly inside as I take a good look around. I'm on a ship, right in the middle of the War of 1812!

Then the reality of that hits me like a soccer ball in the stomach. *I'm on a ship, right in the middle of the War of 1812.*

My mouth goes dry, and I feel a little sick. I clutch the side of the ship, looking down at the water. The deep, cold water—

"Look," Caroline whispers. "See those men? They're marines."

Glad to be distracted, I look at the marines standing stiffly at attention. They wear blue coats with yellow trim and fancy tall hats. Their guns are taller than they are! Caroline tells me that all the other men on board are navy sailors. They wear blue coats, white pants, and black hats.

Caroline bumps her shoulder into mine. "Isn't this exciting? We're on a *navy* ship! Look at that big cannon!" She points at a black cannon on the deck.

I've seen cannons in pictures, but seeing this one up close makes me gulp. "I see it," I say.

An officer snaps a salute at Lieutenant Woolsey. They huddle together, and then the officer begins shouting commands. Sailors scurry about, pulling ropes and raising sails. Soon we're sailing through

the harbor, out to the open lake. If I've made a big mistake by agreeing to this adventure, it's too late to change it now.

 Turn to page 27.

I get up and slowly brush off my shorts and shirt. Even though I know I need to stay here, in my mind I can still see Caroline staring across the water. I bet that once the War of 1812 started, lots of men joined the navy. They were willing to fight so that girls like Caroline wouldn't get their fathers snatched up and taken prisoner. Part of me thinks it must not have done much good, because lots of bad things still happen in the world.

But maybe things would be a whole lot worse without people trying to fight for what's right. People like my mom.

I start walking the familiar path back through the woods, picturing my house in my own time. My throat gets this funny thick feeling, like it does whenever I watch a DVD with some sad parts. I'm going *home.* Even though I wasn't gone for long, I feel as if I've traveled really, really far.

*Well, you **have**,* I realize, feeling like an idiot. I've traveled two hundred years and back. Just thinking about that makes me feel dizzy all over again.

Compared with that, I can't help thinking that Mom being gone on her navy ship for eight months might

not be *quite* as horrible as I've been imagining. At least she'll still be right here in our own time, and I'll be able to talk with her on the phone and on Skype. I bet Mom will feel the same way I do now when she gets back— happy to see her familiar home, but feeling different inside after being away.

I think I'll ask her to take lots of pictures with her digital camera while she's gone. Maybe she can e-mail some to me, and I can take pictures to send back to her. It will help us stay connected while we're apart.

And when she gets home, maybe we can all start planning our next camping adventure. That idea makes me smile.

≥ *The End* ≥

To read this story another way and see how different choices lead to a different ending, go back to page 17.

he compass is still in my hand. I move so that the needle points at me, take a deep breath as the now-familiar dizziness comes over me, and close my eyes.

When I open them again, I'm back beside Lake Ontario. I walk around the bend and see Caroline, still looking out over the lake. She clearly doesn't know I was ever gone.

With a sigh, Caroline turns back to me. "I didn't mean to intrude," she says. "Perhaps you just wanted to be alone. Shall I be on my way?"

"No—please don't go yet," I say. Since I came back to learn more about Caroline, the last thing I want is for her to leave me alone! "I was just, um . . . thinking."

She nods as if that makes perfect sense. "I often come here when I need to think. Lake Ontario can be a comfort, somehow."

I feel the same way about the pond behind our house. But I like my pond because it's little and not very deep. Lake Ontario is so enormous that my heart jumps into my throat every time I look over the water.

"What's that you're holding?" Caroline asks.

I'm glad she interrupted my thoughts. I hold out my palm so that she can see the compass. Then I gasp. That compass is all shiny and sparkly in the sun. It looks brand-new!

Caroline stares at the compass. "Why, Papa has one much like it!" she exclaims. Then her eyes fill with tears.

I blurt out, "Caroline, what happened? How did the British capture your papa?"

"It happened on a fine spring day two months ago." She waves one arm toward the lake. "Papa decided to take a new ship out for a trial sail, and he let me come along. War had been declared, but no one in Sackets Harbor had gotten the news! The British boarded our sloop and captured him. He's being held over there across the lake. The British colony of Upper Canada is just thirty miles away, you know."

Great Britain had colonies in Canada, too? I think. I hadn't known that.

Caroline wipes her eyes and lifts her chin. "Does that compass belong to your papa?" she asks. "Is he in the navy? *So* many navy men are coming into town."

I mumble, "Well, um . . ." I look at my toes. How

am I supposed to answer her questions without telling her where I really came from?

I think hard and pick my next words super carefully. "The compass got passed down in my family. It's a little scary to have a parent in the navy, isn't it."

"My papa isn't actually in the navy," Caroline tells me. "He's a shipbuilder."

Wow! I never thought of anyone actually building a ship.

Then she asks, "Are you planning to look for work in the village? You won't be able to stay at the navy barracks, of course. I expect you'll need to earn some money."

Did some girls our age have real jobs back in 1812? "I—I don't really know what to do next," I confess.

"I have an idea!" Caroline claps her hands together. "You can stay with my family until—"

Boom! Boom-boom! I almost jump out of my skin as the afternoon explodes with a sound like thunder.

"Cannon!" Caroline gasps. She grabs my hand. "Come along! *Run!*"

❀ *Turn to page 31.*

D *on't think about how deep the lake is,* I order myself. *Think about something else.* Looking out over the harbor, I see three canoes paddled by Native Americans. I wish that I knew what tribes lived around here in 1812. Actually, I wish I knew more about *everything* in 1812. "I must admit, being on this ship is pretty cool," I tell Caroline.

She wrinkles her nose, looking confused. "Well, yes," she says, "the breeze does make it feel much cooler on the lake than it was on land. I love it, don't you?" She leans closer. "One day, I shall captain my own ship!"

That surprises me, and I guess it shows, because she adds, "It is my dearest wish, and I *will* make it come true."

"I think you should," I tell her, and she smiles.

Then she gives me a stern look just like her mother did. "While on board, we must stay out of the sailors' way. Hold on to something solid until you're used to the way the ship moves."

"Oh, I'll hold on," I promise.

Since we seem to be out of the way right where we are, I figure I'll just stay put and watch.

This is way better than any movie.

Soon the sails are full and we're moving fast. A U.S. flag with hardly any stars on it is flying in the wind. I guess there weren't very many states in 1812. I'm the only person on board who has any idea how much America will grow and change in the next two hundred years. In fact, I'm the only one who knows that our country survives the War of 1812!

Suddenly I feel a lump in my throat and my eyes fill up with tears. *Oh Mom,* I think. *I don't think I'll ever stop worrying about you sailing on a big navy ship. But I'm starting to get why it's important.*

I slide one hand into my pocket and squeeze the compass Mom gave me. One of my own ancestors fought in the War of 1812! He must have used this very compass on a ship much like this one. When Mom told me about him, it didn't really mean anything. But now, watching these sailors, I feel proud to know that my family helped defend the United States against invasion. Just like members of my family have been proud to serve our country ever since.

"Miss Abbott?" Lieutenant Woolsey calls. "Come meet Sailing Master Adams."

"I must go to the helm and give directions," Caroline says. "Come with me! It's the best place to be on a ship."

Caroline hurries toward the back of the ship. I follow, making my way more slowly. I manage to join Caroline and the two officers without stumbling over my dress, or tripping a sailor by getting in the way, or falling overboard.

Sailing Master Adams stands with arms folded across his chest as Caroline gives directions. He's a head shorter than the lieutenant, but he looks like a strong man used to giving orders. I'm proud of Caroline when she stands tall and describes the secret cove for Sailing Master Adams. He kind of frowns as she talks, and his eyes get real narrow. I wonder if he doesn't like getting instructions from a girl.

Then he nods and says, "Very well, Miss Abbott. I'll head along the shoreline, just as you say." I guess he wasn't mad, just concentrating. He shouts another command.

The sailors are working very hard. They use all their weight and strength when hauling on the ropes that make the sails go up and down. Some of the

men work in the rigging high above the deck. I sure wouldn't want to see any of them fall from up there. At least I know Mom doesn't have to do that when she's on *her* navy ship.

I tell myself I'm having an adventure, and try really hard to enjoy it. The fresh breeze mixes with a whiff of smoke from the pipe that Sailing Master Adams holds clamped between his teeth. One of the sailors begins singing a song I've never heard before. I can't understand all the words, but it sounds cheerful. Caroline nudges me with her elbow and gives me a grin that says, *Isn't this wonderful?*

I manage to smile back. My spirits are actually starting to rise.

Then Lieutenant Woolsey says to the sailing master, "We know British ships are on the prowl, so we must keep a sharp lookout."

That's the end of my rising spirits. The lieutenant's face reminds me just how important—and dangerous—this trip is.

✹ *Turn to page 35.*

I t's hard to run on the stones in this long skirt! I grab up the dress and the petticoat underneath with one hand. Caroline grabs my other hand when I stumble, and I manage to keep going. I guess it's a good thing I'm not wearing sandals anymore— I'd have fallen for sure.

The shoreline curves, and I can see buildings along the shore of a sheltered harbor. There are lots of wooden boats of all sizes there—from rowboats to ships so big that their masts poke up higher than the buildings nearby. One is sailing right out of the harbor, and I can hear the white sails making cracking noises in the breeze. It seems to me that one cannonball could do a lot of damage to a wooden ship! My mom's navy ship would make all of these look like toys, and I'm sure glad she doesn't have to sail away on one of them.

We pound into an area where men are working on a half-built boat. A sign that says "Abbott's" hangs near the street. I can see more houses and buildings on a hill behind the shipyard, but I don't stop to look at them. All I want to do is get away from whatever gun was firing.

Several men are unloading huge logs from a cart.

Hitched to the cart is the biggest cow I've ever seen. It has really long horns. Maybe it's an ox.

A big man with white hair breaks away from the group when Caroline and I tear into the yard. "Here now, Miss Caroline," he calls. "What's all this?"

"Didn't you hear the cannon, Mr. Tate?" she gasps, panting for breath. "Have enemy ships been sighted?"

"No, child, not yet," he says. "The gunners are just practicing."

My shoulders sag. What a relief!

But Mr. Tate continues, "When the enemy comes, the signal guns will keep firing."

I don't feel relieved anymore. The reminder that the enemy might come at any time makes me feel cold from the inside out.

Mr. Tate smiles at me. "Good morning. I don't believe we've met—"

"Look out!" a man at the oxcart shouts. Several enormous logs crash to the ground.

"Tarnation," Mr. Tate mutters. He hurries away. "Have a care there, lads!"

"Mr. Tate is the chief carpenter," Caroline tells me. "Since Papa's away, he's supervising the work here at

our shipyard." She takes my hand again. "Come meet my mother."

"Are we going to your house?" I ask.

She smiles proudly. "Oh, no. Mama is managing the shipyard now."

Caroline leads me inside one of the small buildings in the shipyard. There are books on shelves and drawings of ships tacked up on the wall. A pretty woman is sitting on a high stool, staring at a huge leather book. I can't figure out why she's holding a big feather until she dips it into a little pot of black liquid and writes a number in the ledger. I get it now—she's using a quill pen!

"Mama?" Caroline asks politely.

Mrs. Abbott turns around. Her eyebrows lift in surprise when she sees me. "Well, now," she says. "Who is this?"

"How do you do, ma'am," I say. Should I curtsy? I don't want to mess up, so I make a tiny little bob as I tell her my name.

"She just arrived in Sackets Harbor," Caroline explains. "I said she might stay with us for a day or two."

"I'm happy to help out with chores and things," I add. I can feel sweat running down my face. Away from the lake breeze it is hot, hot, *hot* in here.

"You're welcome to stay at our house, child," Mrs. Abbott says to me. "But are you quite well? You look flushed."

"I'm fine, ma'am." I swipe my hand over my forehead. "Just warm, that's all."

She points at a dipper hanging near the door. "There's a barrel of cool water outside. Get a drink and splash your face, and you'll feel better."

Taking the dipper, I slip out the open door.

"So, what do you know of this girl?" I hear Mama ask Caroline quietly. I pause just by the door. Mom would scold me for eavesdropping, but I really, *really* want to hear what Mrs. Abbott might have to say about me.

✸ *Turn to page 39.*

aroline and I find a place where we can sit on the deck in the sun, out of the way but close enough to hear Sailing Master Adams. I'm watching the men work when suddenly I see someone scamper through a hatchway onto the deck.

It's a little boy! He can't be more than seven years old, but he's lugging a bucket of water. He gets down on his hands and knees and begins scrubbing one corner of the deck with a flat stone. He's so energetic that I can hear the rough scraping sound. He's barefoot, and his long brown hair is tied behind his neck in a ponytail.

I point. "Caroline, look how young that boy is!"

"Oh," she says calmly, "he must be a powder monkey."

"A *what*?"

She laughs. "Well, the proper term is 'ship's boy.' But everyone calls them powder monkeys."

Now I'm totally confused. "Why?"

"When a battle begins, the boys carry gunpowder to the gun crews," she says.

"Such little boys?" My voice comes out kind of squeaky.

Caroline watches the powder monkey work. "I talked with one once. His parents had died, and he had nowhere else to go. He said the sailors look out for him, and he was happy—and proud—to serve on a navy ship."

I squeeze the compass in my pocket, wondering again about my ancestor who served on a ship during the War of 1812. I'd just assumed he was a sailor, or maybe even an officer like Sailing Master Adams. But maybe he was a kid no older than me.

"Miss Caroline!" Sailing Master Adams calls. "I believe we're approaching the spot."

Caroline scrambles to her feet. "Yes sir," she shouts. "Just ease around that bend, and you'll see the opening to the hidden cove."

When I stand up, I see exactly what she's talking about. The shoreline is covered by forest, with mucky-looking marshes along the edge. Ahead of us is a little natural bay, protected by a fishhook of land that curves out into the lake. As we ease into the hidden harbor, even a modern landlubber like me can tell that any passing British ship wouldn't see us until it was too late to escape.

"It's perfect! Good job, Caroline!" I grin at her. It's awesome that she's actually helped Lieutenant Woolsey lay a trap for the British!

She beams. "I can hardly wait to tell Papa. When he gets home, I'll—"

A shout interrupts her. I jerk around and see Lieutenant Woolsey holding a brass spyglass against his right eye. Caroline and I exchange a startled look and creep closer. Squinting, I see a ship in the distance.

"Is it a British ship?" Caroline asks anxiously.

I swallow hard, thinking, *Please say no.*

The lieutenant lowers the spyglass. His eyes have narrowed in a way that reminds me of my cat stalking a mouse in our basement. "It's British, all right," he mutters. "Sailing Master Adams! We shall give chase!"

"But—sir!" Sailing Master Adams cocks his head at Caroline and me. "What about the young ladies?"

Lieutenant Woolsey blinks at us, as if he'd totally forgotten we were there. "Yes, of course," he says. He calls another navy man over. "Take Miss Abbott and her friend ashore. *Quickly!* We must move with haste or we'll lose that British ship!"

"There's no need to take us ashore," Caroline protests. "You'll waste precious time. Please, sir— you *must* show that British ship who rules the lake!"

The lieutenant is peering through his spyglass again. "Miss Abbott, I must put you ashore. It's not safe for you here."

"Sir, we must give chase!" Caroline cries. "We *must*!"

⚙ *To agree with Caroline,*
   turn to page 43.

⚙ *To agree with Lieutenant Woolsey,*
   turn to page 46.

I think her papa is in the navy," Caroline says. "She must have no other family, since she's on her own. She'll need to find work, but I thought that for a few days at least she might stay with us."

"You have a good heart, Caroline," Mrs. Abbott says. "If the poor girl traveled overland, it's no wonder she looks worn. We'll see to her until she can settle herself. She'll be good company for you."

"Perhaps she can help us here," Caroline adds.

I wonder what she just volunteered me for. I don't know one single thing about shipyards! Still, I'm relieved that Mrs. Abbott doesn't seem suspicious about me.

I gulp some water from a tub that looks like a wooden barrel sawed in half. Just as I'm wiping my cheeks, a young man hurries into the shipyard. Unlike Mr. Tate and the other workers at Abbott's, this man wears a uniform. Gold lace, buttons, and braid trim his blue coat. The uniforms in my time look different, but still, I can tell this is an officer in the U.S. Navy.

The officer hurries into the building without even noticing me. I bite my lip. What's he doing here?

I follow him inside and go stand by Caroline.

"Why—Lieutenant Woolsey!" Mrs. Abbott says. She stands up. "I didn't expect you today, sir. Have you a question about the gunboat we're building for you?"

"No, ma'am." Lieutenant Woolsey takes off his hat. He has curly hair combed back from his face, and funny-looking sideburns. "I hope you can help me solve a problem."

I glance at Caroline. She gives me a tiny shrug, as if to say, *I have no idea what he wants.*

"Shortly before Mr. Abbott was captured," Lieutenant Woolsey says, "he told me about a cove he thought would be a perfect hiding spot for one of our ships. We could lie in wait there to ambush and capture any British vessel that dares cross to our side of the lake. He said this hidden cove is near a place he calls Mallard Bay."

Mrs. Abbott nods. "Mallard Bay was—it *is*—his favorite fishing spot."

"It's a wide, marshy bay just a few miles east of here, sir," Caroline adds. She sounds excited. "And not too far from there, the shoreline curves like a hook and makes the little cove. If a ship sailed into that cove, it could hide quite nicely behind the trees."

"Yes, that's just what your father said." Lieutenant Woolsey grips his hat tightly. "He said the little cove is deeper than it looks—deep enough for a schooner. But no one else I've spoken with seems to know exactly where it is."

The lieutenant looks at Caroline's mother. "Mrs. Abbott, I have a schooner waiting. Would you be willing to sail out with my crew and show us the exact location? It may prove vital in our efforts to protect our shore."

"I'm glad to help," she says. "But I've only been to Mallard Bay once or twice, and I don't recall my husband showing me the hiding spot you describe. I'm sure I could find it, given time, but—"

Before she can finish, more shouts from the shipyard drift through the open door. Mrs. Abbott glances out the window, then back at the lieutenant. She looks frazzled, like my mom does when both of the twins are acting up and the phone rings at the same time. "Might we delay the trip for an hour or so, Lieutenant Woolsey?" she asks. "I must be here to take delivery of sailcloth this morning, and Mr. Tate has his hands full."

The lieutenant turns the hat in his hands, as if he has a lot of nervous energy. "I'm eager to get one of my ships into that cove. A new enemy ship might try to sneak close to Sackets Harbor at any moment."

I can feel Caroline quivering anxiously beside me. "We can't let that happen!" she cries. "I know the spot quite well, Mama. *I* could show the way."

✸ *Turn to page 44.*

aroline turns to me, and her excitement washes over me like a big wave. My heart feels like it's beating a million times too fast, but no way am I going to start whining now. "Yes, give chase!" I cry. "Let's chase that ship all the way back to Canada!"

Lieutenant Woolsey snaps an order at Sailing Master Adams. The morning rings with shouted commands. The sailors run to obey their orders. Our ship heaves beneath my feet and changes course. Caroline grabs me and I half sit, half fall onto the deck.

"We must catch them," Caroline murmurs. She hunkers down too, keeping a sharp eye on the enemy. "I want our men to capture that ship!"

Capture that ship? I figured we would just chase the British ship away from the American side of Lake Ontario. I hadn't imagined that we'd actually try to capture it. I don't think the British will just put their hands in the air and say *OK, you win.* I'm pretty sure they'll put up a fight.

"Come about!" Sailing Master Adams shouts.

"Hang on," Caroline warns me.

⊛ *Turn to page 51.*

Mrs. Abbott pinches her mouth tight. "Lieutenant, our village was attacked yesterday," she says at last. "Would Caroline be safe aboard a navy ship today?"

"I give you my word that I will do everything possible to protect Miss Caroline," Lieutenant Woolsey says.

I notice he hasn't actually promised Mrs. Abbott that it's safe to board a navy ship. A shiver slides down my neck like an ice cube.

Mrs. Abbott frowns at a streak of black ink staining one finger as she considers. Finally she looks at her daughter. "Caroline, you made good decisions yesterday and helped our men win the battle. Since one of us must remain at the shipyard, I'll leave this choice to you. Would you rather go with Lieutenant Woolsey, or stay here and take delivery of the sailcloth while I go?"

"I want to help Lieutenant Woolsey!" Caroline says at once, bouncing on her toes. Just when I'm wondering if she's forgotten I'm even here, Caroline turns to me. "Will you come too?"

Suddenly everyone is staring at me. Lieutenant

Woolsey twiddles his hat impatiently. Mrs. Abbott looks concerned, but determined too. Caroline's eyes are dancing with anticipation.

I can see how badly she wants me to say yes. I know that going on the navy ship with Caroline and Lieutenant Woolsey would be an awesome adventure. But it would also mean going out on that huge lake in a creaky wooden boat, and I'm not sure I'm that brave—especially when enemy ships might be prowling nearby!

❈ *To sail on a navy ship,*
   turn to page 18.

❈ *To stay at the shipyard,*
   turn to page 50.

I know Caroline doesn't want to do anything that will slow down the chase for even a minute. But we're on a navy ship that's heading for the enemy! We should not be here. No way.

"We can't stay on this ship," I tell Caroline.

For a moment I think she's going to argue. Then her shoulders droop and she says, "You're right. We should go ashore."

The sailors lower a small rowboat and throw this flimsy little ladder over the side of the schooner. I manage to climb down without falling into the lake. Once we're settled, the sailor quickly rows us away from the ship, leaning back and forth with the effort. I focus on the shore, trying not to look at that dark cold water.

When we reach the marshy shoreline, the sailor threads the boat through the weeds and cattails. "How about that flat rock to land on, if you please?" he asks, pointing. "Should be easy enough to keep your feet dry."

"Perfect," Caroline agrees quietly.

Two minutes later we're both safely landed on the flat rock. "Just give me a moment to hide the boat,"

the sailor says, "and I'll escort you young ladies home."

"*No,*" Caroline says. It comes out sounding almost rude, and I shoot her a glance. Something is wrong, but I don't know what.

Caroline's cheeks get pink. "I mean—thank you, but there's no need to see us home. I know the way perfectly well."

The sailor glances at his ship with longing. I can tell he'd much rather rejoin his crew than stay with us. "If you're certain . . ."

"We're certain," I say firmly. I've already disappointed Caroline once by insisting that we come ashore instead of staying aboard for the chase. I don't want to make things worse.

"Very well, then," he says. He uses one oar to push away from shallow water. Caroline and I watch him make his way back to the open lake.

Once he's gone, the shoreline is quiet. I hear a couple of blackbirds calling, but that's about it. Caroline is staring at a marshy little cove near the entrance to the larger bay.

"I hope you're not angry at me," I say. I'm *very* glad to be back on shore, but her silence is starting to get

to me. Is she mad because I wouldn't stay on the ship when it chased the British?

"No, I think you were right," Caroline says. "We might have gotten in the way if we'd stayed on board."

She's still not looking at me. I sidestep so that I can see her face. The sadness in her eyes hurts my heart. "Caroline?" I ask. "What's wrong?"

"My papa's fish camp is right over there." She blinks hard as tears well in her eyes. "I haven't visited it since he was captured."

"Oh." I don't know what to say.

Caroline finally looks away from the fish camp and blows out a long sigh. "Well, the trail that runs along the lakeshore is nearby. Shall we head home?"

I hesitate. I can tell she's missing her father terribly. Missing a parent is something I understand. I haven't really talked about it with even my best friends, because none of them have parents in the military. I guess I've been afraid they couldn't really get how I feel. But I have a pretty good idea what Caroline is going through, and I know it doesn't feel good to hold things like that inside. Maybe I should try to talk with her about her dad.

On the other hand, I'm afraid she might not want to discuss something so personal with somebody she just met. Maybe I should get Caroline away from here as fast as I can so that she can leave the memories behind.

 To talk with Caroline about Papa,
turn to page 60.

 To hurry Caroline away from the fish camp,
turn to page 77.

I 'd better stay here," I tell Caroline. Disappointment floods her blue eyes. That makes me feel pretty miserable. She's been so friendly that I hate to let her down. Maybe I should just take a walk and do the compass thing and get back to my own time . . .

Then Caroline squares her shoulders. "Mama, you go with Lieutenant Woolsey. I'll stay here and wait for the sailcloth."

My mouth opens in surprise. I didn't mean for Caroline to miss out just so I wouldn't be left alone! I can hardly believe how nice she is.

Mrs. Abbott grabs her bonnet and the shawl hanging on a peg, and then follows the lieutenant out the door.

Caroline grins at me. "Don't worry," she says. "We'll find something fun to do after the sailcloth is delivered, I promise."

I can't help laughing. I have a feeling Caroline finds excitement wherever she goes. And if I hang around with her, I'd better be ready for some adventures!

⊛ *Turn to page 54.*

T he ship shudders, and the sails snap in the wind. I've found a wooden bar to hold on to, and I close my eyes and hang on tight as the ship leans way, way over on one side. I want to scream "We're going to capsize!" but my teeth are clenched. Finally, just when I'm sure I'm about to drown, the ship swings up straight again.

"What happened?" I gasp. "What's wrong with the ship?"

"Nothing," Caroline says. "We had to make a hard turn, that's all."

I should never have agreed to this! My arms feel bruised from hanging on to the bar, but I can't bring myself to let go.

"Sir!" one of the men shouts. "They're turning about!"

"The British must have realized they can't outrun us," Caroline mutters.

"What does that mean?" I demand, although I don't think I want to know the answer.

Lieutenant Woolsey nods with a look of grim satisfaction. "Well," he says, "if it's a fight they want, it's a fight they'll get."

"A fight?" I squawk. I can hardly breathe. Looking around the deck, I realize that the little powder monkey is nowhere in sight. Has he gone below? Is he getting ready for battle?

Caroline's eyes are wide. I can tell she's scared too. But she also looks really stubborn. For her, this is personal.

Boom! The sound seems to tremble over the water. A puff of smoke appears in the air by the British ship. The British have fired a cannonball! I start feeling like I might throw up. How could I have agreed to stay on board and chase an enemy ship?

Nearby, several sailors are frantically working to load one of our cannons. When it fires, the explosion is so loud that I let go of the bar and clap my hands over my ears. The men jump away as the heavy cannon jerks backward, but quick as a blink they get back to work. "Where's the blasted boy?" one of them shouts.

Caroline and I cling to each other. After a moment, though, she pulls away. Her face is white, but she's obviously thinking clearly instead of panicking like me. "Do you wish to go below? Would you prefer not to watch?"

I almost shout, *I don't **know**!* But I take a deep breath and try to think. Would I feel safer below, or just trapped? Should we hide, or stay where we are and face the enemy?

⊕ *To go below,*
   turn to page 58.

⊕ *To stay up on deck,*
   turn to page 68.

aroline begins tidying the office, and I grab a dust rag and pitch in. Maybe fifteen minutes later, someone knocks on the door. A dark-haired guy only a few years older than me pokes his head inside. He's wearing a stained shirt and trousers, and he's barefoot. "Pardon me, miss," he says to Caroline. His words are polite, but his tone isn't. "Is Mrs. Abbott about? A delivery wagon just turned in."

He's not paying attention to me, but I frown at him anyway. He's got a sort of scornful look on his face, and I don't like it.

Caroline stands very straight and looks him in the eye. "I am expecting a delivery of sailcloth," she tells him firmly. "Please send the driver here."

After he leaves, I turn to Caroline. "Who was that?"

She sighs. "That's Jed. He's one of our woodworkers."

A barefoot woodworker? I can just hear my parents lecturing about safety, and how important it is to wear good shoes.

"I don't think Jed likes having Mama in charge of the shipyard, instead of a man," Caroline adds.

Tough luck, Jed! I think. It's kind of weird—I already feel loyal to Caroline and her mother, even though

I just met them. I tell Caroline, "Well, he'll just have
to deal with it."

"I beg your pardon?" Caroline looks confused.

Maybe people didn't say "deal with it" two hundred years ago. Before I can figure out what to say
next, the driver arrives in the doorway. "Want to check
the delivery?" he calls.

I follow Caroline outside to the driver's wagon.
A big black horse stands patiently in its harness in front
of the wagon, which is half full of crates and barrels.
Piles of folded pale canvas fill the rest of the wagon.

Caroline counts the big pieces of canvas while the
driver unloads them. "Just as we ordered," she says.
"Jed, would you please fetch Hosea?"

Jed twists his mouth, gives Caroline one short nod,
and trots away. He sure doesn't like taking directions
from a girl. *Tough luck, Jed!* I think again, and put my
hand over my mouth to hide a smile. Jed seems like
a royal pain to me.

Jed soon returns with a black man who has a soft
voice and a kind smile. Caroline introduces him as
Hosea, the sailmaker.

Hosea fingers some of the canvas before telling

Caroline, "This is good quality, miss. I'm satisfied."

"Very well," Caroline says. She calls two more workers over to help carry the canvas to Hosea's workshop. Then she sends the deliveryman on his way.

I am super impressed with the way Caroline handles everything. The only "business" I ever tried to do was selling Girl Scout cookies. Everybody I talked to was either a neighbor or a relative, and it was *still* hard.

Caroline carefully records the delivery in the big ledger in the office. Then she grins at me. "Well," she says, "that's taken care of. Would you like to see the rest of the shipyard?"

I grin. "Yes, I'd love to!"

Caroline shows me where two men are using a really long saw to slice tree trunks into planks. One of the men is standing in a waist-deep pit and holding his end of the saw from there. It seems weird, but she says it's the best way. It looks like a huge job! I'd never really thought about how hard it was to do work like that without power tools.

"Your mom—um, I mean your mother—mentioned that you're making a gunboat for the navy," I say.

I point across the yard to the half-built boat I noticed earlier. "Is that it? Will the planks the men are sawing be used in a gunboat?"

"Yes to both questions," Caroline says proudly. "The navy is counting on us to help them."

I have about a thousand questions, but before I can ask any, Mr. Tate approaches. His eyes are sparkling, although I'm not sure why. "Now that the sailcloth has been delivered, would you like to take the skiff out? It's a fine day with a fair wind."

I don't know what a skiff is, but I'm pretty sure he's talking about going sailing on Lake Ontario. I can't believe my bad luck—the thought of sailing on this lake in a little wooden ship is like something out of my worst nightmare.

❂ *Turn to page 64.*

L et's go down!" I shout.

Caroline nods and takes a deep breath. "Follow me!" She scurries to the closest little hatchway.

I'm shaking so hard that I'm not sure my legs will work, but somehow I manage to scramble after her. I trip on the steep little ladder and fall down the last two steps, landing in a heap and banging my elbow so hard that tears come to my eyes.

A man races around a corner and almost stumbles over me. "Out of the way!" he bellows. I squeeze against one wall in the narrow passageway as he tears by.

A second sailor is right behind the first. "First the boy disappears, and now we have little girls underfoot!" he snaps, glaring at Caroline and me.

"I—we're sorry, sir," Caroline stammers, but the men have already pounded up the steps.

"Did he say the boy disappeared?" I ask. My nerves are so jittery that I'm not sure I heard right.

Caroline turns to me with a look of despair. "He must mean the powder monkey!"

"Where could he have gone?" I ask.

"I don't know," Caroline says grimly. "But without the powder monkey to fetch ammunition, men will

have to leave their guns to fetch it themselves." She nibbles her bottom lip. "Maybe we should look for him. If he's not up on deck, he must be down here."

Another *boom* sounds. The whole ship shudders. Men are roaring orders and taunts, and running back and forth. "Well, I guess we can look around a little," I say. My voice is shaking as badly as the ship.

"All right," Caroline says. Her voice is shaky too. She grabs my hand and we set off.

There aren't that many hiding places where we can search. Caroline leads me into a tiny kitchen with a little black stove and a table. Wooden dishes are tucked behind safety rails on shelves. Kettles, a bucket, and a lantern swing from the ceiling.

"Is this—" I begin, but Caroline puts a finger over her lips to say *Shhh. Listen.*

✸ *Turn to page 75.*

O K, here goes. "Caroline, do you want to show me your father's fish camp before we go?" I ask.

Caroline looks startled. She hesitates, and wipes a stray tear from her cheek. "I don't know if I want to go there," she says slowly. "Perhaps we could just sit here for a little while?"

We plop down. The sun has warmed the rock nicely, and I draw up my knees under my skirt. "What's your father like?" I ask.

Caroline smiles. "He teaches me about sailing, and takes me skating in the winter, and—and all kinds of things." Her words come in an avalanche. "He brought my cat Inkpot home for me, and he gave me the most beautiful sewing cabinet you can imagine, and he taught me how to tie sailors' knots."

"He sounds really special," I say. "I wish I could meet him."

"I hope you will, one day soon," Caroline declares. She seems a little less sad now.

"Caroline, I wanted to tell you that I was really impressed when you said you wanted to stay on board the ship while Lieutenant Woolsey chased the British," I say. "Don't you *ever* get scared?"

Caroline looks surprised. "I get scared all the
time. When the British captured Papa and our sloop,
I had to get into a small boat with an enemy officer
who promised to take me back to Sackets Harbor.
I told Papa I didn't want to go with the British,
but he said I had to be brave and obey. I think . . ."
She pauses. "I think I learned that day that sometimes you have to do really hard things even if you
are afraid."

"Yes." I sigh, thinking about saying good-bye
to Mom. "Sometimes that's what you have to do."

Caroline gives me a little smile. "One day, when
Papa comes home, I want people to tell him that
I stayed steady." She gazes toward the horizon.

All of a sudden, I'm just about to burst. I want
to share with her, just like she's sharing with me.

"Caroline," I blurt out, "my mother is—she's in
the U.S. Navy."

Caroline stares at me. Finally she says, "Your
mother? In the *navy*? You mean . . . she's disguised
herself as a man?"

"Something like that." I hold my breath. If Caroline
says anything mean about my mom, I don't think I'll

be able to stand it. I slide my hand into my pocket and clench the compass.

But very slowly, a delighted smile spreads over her face. "I've heard of women doing that, but I didn't quite believe it. Oh my. I do so hope I might meet her one day! I'll tell her I think she's very, *very* brave," Caroline adds earnestly.

Have I ever told Mom that *I* think she's very, very brave? Actually, I'm sure I've never gotten around to saying anything like that. My cheeks grow warm with shame.

"You know what?" I say. "I'll tell her for you, first chance I get." And suddenly, I want that "first chance" to come quickly. I've made a true friend here in 1812, but it's time to go home.

Caroline nods. "Are you trying to find her? No wonder you sounded so confused when I found you on the shore earlier! You didn't know how to explain, right?"

I almost start to laugh at that. "That's right," I admit. "I didn't have any *idea* how to explain."

"I promise I'll keep your secret," Caroline says. "I'll never tell anyone about your mother."

"Thank you," I say. I'm pretty sure I'll have to keep Caroline a secret from my friends and family, too.

That doesn't matter, though. She's helped me do some unbelievable things. And who knows? Maybe one day I'll use the compass to come back to 1812. I'd like that a lot, and I think Caroline would too.

Now, though, I need to go home and clean up some of my mistakes. I've figured out that being brave doesn't really mean never being afraid. Being brave is about doing what you need to do even if you are frightened. My mom might be a little scared about going to sea. Dad never shows that he's worried about Mom leaving on her navy ship, but I bet he is deep down inside. They're both probably just better than I am about dealing with it. They're doing what they need to do.

When I get home, I'm going to try to do a better job of doing what *I* need to do, too.

≥ The End ≤

To read this story another way and see how different choices lead to a different ending, go back to page 49.

C aroline catches her breath. "May we truly?" She's bouncing up and down again. "Oh, thank you, Mr. Tate! We'll be ever so careful, I promise."

The big man laughs. "I know you will, Miss Caroline. Just keep an eye on the sky—you know how fast storms can blow in. I'll have a couple of the men bring *Sparrow* out of the shed. Have fun!"

Ten minutes later, I'm standing on the shipyard dock, staring at the small, *small* boat tied to a piling. It's hardly more than a rowboat. My stomach feels sloshy. "Um . . . are you sure it's safe for us to go sailing in that?" I ask.

"Of course!" Caroline says indignantly. "There's no finer boat on the whole lake. My papa built this skiff, and he taught me to be a good sailor."

My mouth feels dry as paper. Caroline might have a lot of sailing experience, but she's just a kid! Besides, I don't see any life jackets anywhere. My mom would ground me for a million years if she knew I went sailing without one. I hate to disappoint Caroline *again,* but I have to. "Caroline?" I say. "The thing is, I—"

"Caroline!" someone hollers. Footsteps come pounding down the dock. I whirl and see a tall, skinny

teenage boy running toward us. He's gasping for breath. "I'm—so glad—I caught you!"

"Seth, what's wrong?" Caroline cries.

"Nothing." He grins at her, and I can tell that these two are good friends. "I just heard that some men northeast of here are going to attack the British fort on Pine Island. I want to join them, but time is short! Can you—"

"Of course we'll take you!" Caroline exclaims. She turns to me and tugs my arm. "Quick—get into the skiff!"

I find myself being hurried down a wooden ladder into the skiff. Believe me, going down a ladder in a long dress is not easy. But Caroline and her friend are coming down right after me, so I need to keep moving or get stepped on. The skiff bobs, and I half fall onto a plank seat. I grab hold with both hands and hang on.

Seth takes another seat, settles two long oars into place, and begins to row through the harbor. "I'm Seth, by the way," he says to me.

I introduce myself. My voice sounds as wobbly as I feel.

"Seth's the local mail walker," Caroline adds.

"We've been friends forever."

"I'm not sure about this," I say. "I—I don't want to do anything dangerous." Like sailing into an ocean-sized lake in a skiff that's hardly bigger than my bathtub!

Seth misunderstands me. "I don't think the raid will be very dangerous," he says. "Captain Miller put the plan together, and I trust his judgment. And you girls don't need to do more than drop me off at Miller's place. I can walk home after the raid."

"I'd love to see a British soldier or two taken prisoner," Caroline declares.

OK, I think, *this is bad.*

"Hold the oars, Seth," Caroline says. "I'm going to raise the sail."

My heart races. Facing my fear of water is bad enough. Getting anywhere close to a raid on a British fort is way, way worse.

You chose to come back to 1812 and make sure Caroline was OK, says one side of my mind. *You're here now, so you need to help the Americans win the war!* If Mom ever got captured and held as a prisoner by enemy soldiers, I'd want to do everything possible to help win the

war—and win her freedom. Caroline's papa is being held by the British, and Seth's news has given her a chance to do something to beat them. It would break her heart if I insisted we turn back now. I have to see this through.

But there's another voice in my mind—a scared, modern voice that says, *You need to be responsible and remember all the things Mom and Dad have taught you. You have to tell Caroline and Seth that you won't go sailing toward a raid!*

✹ *To help Seth get to the raid,*
  turn to page 70.

✹ *To insist on a different plan,*
  turn to page 92.

There's so much noise that I have to shout into Caroline's ear to be heard. "Let's stay up here!"

She's trembling, but she gives one sharp nod. "At least we can see what's happening," she agrees.

We huddle together, trying to stay out of the way as the sailors pound back and forth. The officers are bellowing orders. Our ship fires another cannonball, and the deafening explosion makes my ears ring. I hang on as we change course.

The British ship comes back into view. We're close enough to see the enemy flag flying, and men on the deck, and black guns poking out of the ship's sides. *I'm in the middle of a battle!* I think. It almost feels like a bad dream. Mom and Dad would be so upset if they knew where I was. Should I use the compass to get out of here?

No, I decide. Even though I'm so scared that I might throw up, I know I can't zip out of here right now. What would Caroline think if I just disappeared? What if the sailors got distracted, right when they needed to concentrate on their work?

OK, I tell myself. *I have to make good choices and stay safe until this is over.*

The British ship fires again, and a cannonball hits one of our masts. Bits of wood explode, and I cover my face with my hands. But when one of the sailors screams, I peek between my fingers. I'm horrified to see that a young man has fallen to the deck nearby. He's clutching his left shoulder with his right hand. Blood is staining his shirt a rusty red.

"That sailor is wounded!" Caroline gasps.

The sailor crawls out of the path of pounding feet before collapsing on the deck. None of the other sailors pay any attention to him. *They all have a job to do right now,* I realize. *That poor guy is on his own until the fight is finished.*

I can't bear the thought of that. "Come on, Caroline! Let's see if we can help."

❋ *Turn to page 129.*

I grit my teeth and hold in my worries while Caroline gets the sail up. At least we're sailing near the shoreline. Looking at land is better than staring out over the restless water.

We don't pass any other towns or villages as we sail along. Most of the land here is covered with the biggest trees I've ever seen. I imagine that Native American people live around here somewhere, but I don't see any.

"Look ahead." Caroline gestures toward a few little wooded islands in the distance. "There are hundreds of islands in this direction."

"Pine Island, the one with the British fort, is so close to the American shore that Captain Miller can see it from his cabin," Seth adds. "He hates knowing that the British can spy on every passing American ship. That's why he wants to capture the fort—and he'll do it, too! He fought in the Revolution, so he's got experience."

In school we learned how hard the Patriots fought to win independence for the United States of America. It would be amazing to actually meet a Patriot soldier from the Revolutionary War!

After a while Seth points toward a clearing on the American shore. "There's Captain Miller's landing," he says. "Let's drop the sail."

Caroline lowers the sail, and Seth rows toward a clearing in the thick forest along the shore. I can see three log buildings, and a few people clustered on the beach. I feel enormous relief when we reach shallow water. Gravel scrapes beneath the skiff. Seth jumps out, not seeming to care that his shoes get wet, and hauls our skiff up on shore. Then he holds out a hand to me. I need his help to reach dry land. Caroline scampers out on her own.

A short man with a long gray beard and a face full of wrinkles comes to meet us. "Seth Whittleslee!" he exclaims. "Have you come to join us?" He gestures behind him, but the only people I see are two men who look like farmers and a boy who's younger than me. Where is the force that's going to attack the British fort?

"Yes, Captain Miller," Seth says proudly. "I got word of your plan in Sackets Harbor and came in all haste."

"Good thing you did so," Captain Miller says gruffly. "We're about to depart. If word's reached

Sackets already, we must move now, before the blasted British know what we're up to."

A question just pops out of my mouth: "But where are the soldiers?" Surely two farmers and a couple of boys aren't enough to attack an enemy fort!

Captain Miller looks at me for the first time. "One Patriot is worth six Redcoats, miss. We proved that when we won independence thirty years ago. Don't you forget it."

This man actually fought in the Revolutionary War, I remind myself. I still don't understand what I'm doing here in 1812, but meeting this guy is awesome. "Yes, sir," I say.

"I'm glad you've brought a skiff," Captain Miller tells Seth. "My own skiff couldn't have gotten my men and me across in one trip."

Seth clears his throat. "Actually, sir, the skiff belongs to Miss Abbott here, not me. I told these girls they could head home after dropping me off here."

Captain Miller turns to me and Caroline and barks, "We need the skiff! You girls will have to walk home."

Caroline's eyes get narrow, like she's thinking.

Then she says, "Or we could go along, and watch the boats while you capture the fort."

"*What?*" I screech.

Captain Miller drowns me out. "Get on home with you, Miss Abbott." He turns away and starts giving instructions to the two farmers, Seth, and the little boy.

"What are you thinking?" I whisper fiercely to Caroline.

She flaps a hand at me. "*Shhh!*"

Captain Miller paces back and forth. "I've been watching the British force on Pine Island for a week," he tells Seth and the others. "I doubt that there's more than half a dozen men over there."

Half a dozen British soldiers? Only *six*? I'd been imagining hundreds of them!

"He's letting that little boy go on the raid," Caroline hisses to me. "The only reason he won't let us go is that we're girls."

"Girls can do anything boys can do," I agree automatically. My mom has helped prove that women can serve just fine in the navy, and that's how I'm used to thinking.

That's all Caroline needs to hear. "I'm going to talk to Captain Miller again."

I grab her arm. "Caroline, wait." Learning that there are only a few British soldiers on Pine Island makes the raid sound a lot less scary. But still . . . it could be dangerous. I understand why Caroline wants to help, but is it too risky?

❀ *To go on the raid,*
   turn to page 82.

❀ *To head home,*
   turn to page 84.

I listen. At first I don't hear anything but men shouting and one more *boom*. Then my ears catch the sound that Caroline heard: a soft hiccuping sniffle.

Caroline cocks her head toward some wooden crates and kegs stacked on the floor. One seems to be out of place. We tiptoe over and peek behind the crates—and there's the boy, sitting on the floor, knees tucked up. When he spots us, his eyes go round with alarm.

"Don't be frightened," Caroline says quickly.

"Not of us, at least," I add, since I don't expect the boy to stop being scared of cannonballs. "Are you all right? What's your name?"

"Zeke," he whispers. He blinks tears away, wipes his nose on his sleeve, and climbs to his feet. "I'm in big trouble. I'm supposed to be helping the men. But when the firing started, I—I . . ." His voice trails away.

"You got scared?" I guess. "Don't feel bad. I'm really scared too."

Caroline asks, "Is this your first battle?"

The boy rubs one bare toe against the floor. "Yes. But we've practiced and *practiced*. I know what

to do. I just . . . I found myself hiding instead of doing my duty."

Will he be punished for hiding? The poor kid looks terrified.

Caroline grabs Zeke's arm. "Come along," she says. "It's not too late to set things right. Where are you supposed to be?" She tugs him from behind the crates and gives him a little push. And that does the trick, as my dad would say. The boy hurries from the kitchen.

He leads us down a passageway into a big open space and points to a corner where blankets are hung from the ceiling. "There," he says.

"What's with the blankets?" I can't help asking.

"We hang wet blankets around the powder supply," he explains. He has stopped crying, and his voice has grown stronger. "To help keep stray sparks from exploding the powder."

Our *own* supply of gunpowder might explode? Suddenly my knees feel like pudding. As if having the British shoot cannonballs at us isn't enough!

✸ *Turn to page 98.*

Y es, let's head back to Sackets Harbor," I say. "I imagine you have lots to do."

"There are always chores waiting," Caroline agrees. She takes one last look toward her father's fish camp and then turns away. "If my grandmother were here, she'd say there's nothing to gain from moping about."

I can't help smiling. "That sounds like something my mother would say."

We start into the woods. It seems like we've gone a very long way when Caroline says, "Let's walk a little faster. Have you noticed the clouds moving in? It looks as if it might rain."

"I hadn't noticed," I admit. I've been totally focused on the trail—it's pretty rough, and my shoes slip a lot more than the hiking shoes I have in my own time. Now I look up through the tree branches and glimpse dark clouds. "Good thing you're paying attention."

She shrugs. "My papa taught me to always watch the weather. That's what sailors do. The habit has saved me from getting soaked more than once."

"In a way, it's like your papa's still here helping you," I say.

"I like that idea." Caroline smiles.

Is there something special Mom taught me? I wonder. *Something I can keep doing after she's gone to sea?*

For a moment I feel terrible, because I can't think of anything. Then a picture pops into my head: me and Mom making snickerdoodle cookies together. When I was really little, she did almost everything. Now I can mix and bake them all by myself, and she mostly just keeps me company.

I decide I'll make snickerdoodles every single week while she's gone. I can even mail some to her for a nice surprise.

Then another idea comes to my mind. Making snickerdoodles is a special thing I do with Mom, but it might be time to share it with my sisters. Sasha and Britney are old enough to start helping in the kitchen. Everything will take ten times longer and they'll probably make a big mess, but as long as I allow extra time, it will be fun. Making cookies can be something special they do with *me.*

Thinking about snickerdoodles reminds me that we haven't had lunch, so I'm glad when we stop at a cabin in a small clearing. A girl gives us some cornbread and dried fish to munch.

"It was nice of her to give us food," I tell Caroline as we get back on the trail. "Is she a friend?"

Caroline shakes her head. "Her family just moved here. She did seem nice, though, didn't she?"

My mouth is full, so I just nod. I like the way people in 1812 seem ready to help travelers out, no questions asked.

Finally the forest thins. We pass through an ugly area where there isn't much but stumps. It looks so raw and forlorn that I can't help wrinkling my nose. "What happened here?"

"You can't imagine how much building has been going on in Sackets Harbor since the war began!" Caroline says. "It used to be a quiet little village, but now we've got hundreds and hundreds of soldiers and sailors, and more arriving every day. We need lots of lumber at the shipyard, and the military men are building lookouts and storehouses—all sorts of things. The sawyers and carpenters have been busy."

I glance back at the thick forest we've just hiked through. In my time, going for a walk in the woods is a special thing. I wonder if Caroline could ever imagine a time when forests are precious.

Soon we're in Sackets Harbor, which is good, because clouds are piling up in big towers. Caroline and I stop at the shipyard to tell her mother why we left the navy ship. Then we climb a hill to the Abbotts' house. It's two stories tall but not very big, with a fence around the lawn and gardens.

Caroline pauses before turning in at the gate. From this spot, we can look down on the harbor. I can see the tall masts sticking up from ships.

"I love being able to see the harbor from here," Caroline says. "I watch it a lot. Sometimes I imagine my papa sailing right in from the lake, coming home."

"I hope he does soon," I tell her. My mom hasn't even left yet, and I'm already imagining the day her ship comes home.

Caroline takes me past a vegetable garden and leads me to the back door. "Grandmother's likely in the kitchen," she explains. I follow Caroline inside, and she introduces me to a small woman with white hair who leans on a cane. Then Caroline turns to me. "This is my grandmother, Mrs. Livingston."

Mrs. Livingston studies me silently for a moment. I try not to squirm, hoping she won't ask too many

questions about me "getting lost." If I fudge the facts even a little bit, I'm pretty sure she'll know I'm not telling the whole truth about where I came from.

 Turn to page 86.

Yes," I tell Caroline. "Let's go on the raid." My heart is thumping, but all I can think about is how I'd feel if Mom was being held prisoner. I'd want to do anything to help get her back.

"Will you come talk to Captain Miller with me?" Caroline whispers.

"Of course," I say. It's kind of nice to know that even Caroline Abbott, who's brave enough to sail a tiny skiff on Lake Ontario, needs a friend when it comes to arguing with a veteran of the Revolutionary War.

We hurry over to the cluster of men and boys. Caroline calls, "Captain Miller?"

"What now?" he snaps. "We've got surprise on our side, but only if we get moving!"

Caroline starts talking really fast. "My friend and I would be honored to sail you to Pine Island. We can wait with the boats while you take the fort. If we don't go, you'll have to beach the skiffs so that they don't float away. We can keep them in shallow water, ready to go in case you need to leave the island quickly."

In case the British chase our men from the fort and try to capture them, she means. I swallow hard.

Captain Miller hesitates, and I can tell that he's

considering Caroline's offer. "Once our attack begins, I'll have no time for girls who weep or faint," he warns.

"Sir, you can count on us," I say, before I have a chance to chicken out. I hope like crazy that I haven't made a humongous mistake.

❀ *Turn to page 112.*

I really think we should just walk back to the village like Captain Miller told us to," I say. "He's an adult, and he's in charge. We'd better do what he says."

Caroline isn't ready to agree. "But—"

"Your mother and Mr. Tate don't even know where we've gone!" I remind her. "Suppose the British soldiers capture the raiding party? If we were waiting by the boats, would they capture us, too?"

"Well . . . I suppose they might," Caroline whispers reluctantly. "And if we just disappeared, my mother would be frantic with worry."

The men pile into the skiffs and head out. Seth gives one last wave before turning toward the island.

"Seth is one of my very best friends," Caroline says. "It's so hard to wave good-bye, not knowing what's going to happen!"

"Don't I know it," I say with a big, big sigh. "Sometimes, though, we have to." I think about my mom leaving. I'll try to make the best of it . . . but that doesn't really help me feel any better. And when I see the sadness in Caroline's eyes, I can tell she feels the same way.

"If my grandmother were here, she'd say there's nothing to gain from moping about," Caroline says. But I can tell by her helpless shrug that she doesn't entirely agree with her grandmother.

It sounds like Caroline's grandmother and my mother have some things in common. Mom has told me over and over that if I start missing her too much while she's away at sea, I just need to keep busy. Since she hasn't left yet, I haven't had a chance to try it, but it seems like a good idea.

"Let's head back to Sackets Harbor," I say. "There must be *something* we can do to help win the war."

"Do you really think so?" Caroline asks.

"Yes," I say firmly. And to my surprise, I discover that I really do believe that. Funny—back when I was feeling so bad about my own mom leaving, I was sure that nothing could help. It wasn't until I started trying to cheer Caroline up that I figured out what might keep me going, too.

✹ *Turn to page 90.*

J ust when I'm about to panic, Caroline's grandmother nods. "Welcome to Sackets Harbor, child," she says. I'm relieved—if she guesses that I have a whopping secret, she isn't going to give me away.

Caroline tells her all about sailing with Lieutenant Woolsey and going ashore after the enemy ship was spotted. While she talks, I study the kitchen. The kettles hanging in the fireplace are made of iron, and I see dishes made from metal—I think they call it pewter?— and china. I'm pretty sure the tall, skinny wooden container in the corner is a butter churn.

When Caroline finishes the tale, she flops down on a bench. "So we don't know if Lieutenant Woolsey captured that British ship or not!"

"We'll hear the news in time," her grandmother says calmly.

"But it's so hard to wait!" Caroline protests. "I *hate* waiting."

Mrs. Livingston looks down her nose at Caroline. "Are you going to sit there and complain?" she asks. "Or are you going to do something useful to help pass the time?"

Caroline blows out a sigh. "I'll do something useful."

"And I'll help," I chime in.

Mrs. Livingston glances toward a small wooden door that's built into the brick wall surrounding the fireplace, about waist high. "I was just about to put my bread into the bake oven."

"Oh Grandmother, I'll do that!" Caroline says quickly. "That door is heavy."

I watch as Caroline lifts a latch on the little door and pulls it clear out. It must be really heavy, because Caroline pinches her mouth with effort. As she sets the door aside, a wave of heat and some smoke blow out of the oven. I try to peer inside, but all I see are a bunch of embers glowing red and gold inside a black cave made of bricks.

"Quickly, now," Mrs. Livingston says. "Or we'll lose all the heat."

Caroline uses something that looks like a garden hoe with a really long handle to scrape all the coals from the brick oven. Right before they'd fall onto the floor, they disappear through a little slot. There's a small door in the wall below, and I guess the embers and ashes will sit in some hidden space until they cool off. *That's how they heat the oven!* I think, as it all starts

to make sense. Mrs. Livingston must have built a fire earlier right inside the oven. Now the bricks are hot enough to bake bread.

"Hand me the peel, would you?" Caroline asks me.

Oh boy, I think. I have *no* idea what she's talking about.

Caroline looks surprised by my ignorance, but she's too polite to say anything. Instead she points to a long-handled wooden paddle leaning against the wall. I pass it over.

Caroline holds the paddle out while her grandmother lifts a cloth from six round lumps of bread dough sitting on the table. At least I'm pretty sure it's bread dough. "You're making six loaves?" I ask. That seems like a whole lot of bread.

Caroline looks even more surprised. "We don't want to heat the oven more than once a week, of course."

Oh, of course! I think. *It's a big, hot job.* My cheeks get warm. I hope they assume it's just from the heat of the oven.

Mrs. Livingston sets two rounds of dough on the paddle. She doesn't use any pans, which seems a little weird, but I don't say anything. With the long-handled

peel, Caroline puts the dough into the bake oven. Once all six loaves are in, Caroline latches the heavy little door back in place.

"There now," Mrs. Livingston says briskly. "We can get some chores done while the bread bakes. Shall we sew?"

"I'd like that," Caroline says. Then she glances at me. "The clouds would make it nice and cool for gardening, though. Maybe we should work outside until the rain starts."

I've done a little sewing, but I don't know if I'd be up to Mrs. Livingston's standards. Then again, I've pulled enough weeds in my family's flower beds to know gardening is hard work, and I'm already tired from our long walk home.

 To stay inside and sew,
turn to page 96.

 To work in the garden,
turn to page 101.

We set out for Sackets Harbor on a narrow footpath that weaves through the woods along Lake Ontario. Most of the time, all I can see is trees and water. Every once in a while we pass a clearing. There's usually a log cabin there, and a little barn or shed. That's it.

Once, we stop to say hello to a woman who is stirring something in a huge iron kettle hanging over a crackling fire. I peek inside and see that she's swishing pieces of cloth back and forth amid a scum of bubbles. All of a sudden I get it: She's doing laundry! Her cheeks are bright red. Sweat runs down her face and stains her dress. I guess I shouldn't complain *too* much about having to help with laundry after Mom leaves. At least we have a washing machine.

The woman gives us some bread and cheese to nibble along the trail. I'm getting really tired by the time Caroline says cheerfully, "Almost home." She leads me down a faint path toward the rocky beach.

I'm still thinking about the woman back at the cabin. Every little chore is so hard in 1812! I don't know if—

Bam! I walk right into Caroline. I hadn't even

noticed that she stopped walking. Before I can say
a word, Caroline shakes her head and puts a finger
over her lips.

Suddenly I see why she stopped. Down on the
beach, a young man has just appeared around a rocky
ledge. He's carrying something that looks sort of like
an ax, but the blade is curved. He walks quickly, with
his head down and his shoulders hunched, like he
doesn't want anybody to notice him. It's hard to get
a good look at him, but he seems familiar . . .

Then I recognize him. It's Jed! Jed, the worker at
Abbott's Shipyard who doesn't like having a woman—
or a girl—in charge. What's he doing sneaking away
from the yard in the middle of the day?

❂ *Turn to page 109.*

L isten," I say, talking really fast so that Caroline and Seth can't interrupt. "This is a bad idea. Seth, I understand why you want to help on the raid. I really do! But it could be terribly dangerous. We should leave the fighting to Captain Miller and his men."

Seth looks unhappy. "But—"

"Please," I beg.

Caroline looks as unhappy as Seth, but she reluctantly nods. "She's my guest," she tells Seth in a low voice. "And she's frightened. We shouldn't have hurried her into the skiff without giving her a chance to say no."

Well, that makes me feel like a big fat fraidy-cat. Still, I know I'm right to make Caroline and Seth call off their crazy plan.

But Seth shakes his head stubbornly. "Let me off, then," he says, pointing toward shore. "I'll walk from here."

"Very well," Caroline says. She maneuvers the skiff toward the shore. In a few minutes Seth splashes overboard into shallow water and scrambles up the bank. "I'll tell you what happens on the raid!" he shouts.

"Take care!" Caroline hollers after him. We wave until he disappears into the trees.

"*Thank* you," I say to Caroline. "I know you only stayed behind because of me." I hold my breath. I haven't known Caroline very long, but I like her so much that I'll feel awful if she's angry with me.

Caroline heaves a very long sigh. "I think you were right," she admits. "Seth's news got me so excited that I didn't think things through. We didn't even talk to Mama or Mr. Tate about where we were going!"

That makes me feel a little better. Maybe being a big fat fraidy-cat isn't always such a bad thing.

Caroline uses one oar to swing the skiff around. "So," she says, "why don't we sail back along the shoreline in the other direction? We can scout for British ships!"

The wind pushes some hair into my face, and while shoving it back I try to think of an answer. Caroline's face has brightened again. I know she wants to do *something* to help win the war—and I can't blame her for that.

Since I've nixed the idea of going on the raid, I figure the least I can do is face my fear of being out

on the water and let Caroline take me sailing. I tell myself it's extremely unlikely that we'll actually spot an enemy ship. The American navy ships are already on the lookout. I take a deep breath and say, "All right. Let's go scouting."

The little skiff zooms over the lake. I clutch the wooden seat so hard that my fingers hurt, but I can't let go. Once, I dare to look over the side. The water is pretty clear, but I can't see the bottom. My stomach is tied in a big knot. I think of Mom, heading out onto the ocean on her navy ship. It's so huge that it needs *really* deep water to travel through. Sometimes I have nightmares about Mom somehow ending up in the ocean. What if she fell overboard and nobody noticed?

OK, I tell myself, *stop thinking about that.*

I try to pay attention to what's happening right here, right now, in 1812. I notice that the wind is picking up and some dark clouds are building in the distance. "Should we head back, do you think?" I ask.

"Oh, not quite yet," Caroline says. She looks happy, and I realize in a new way just how much she loves

skimming over the waves. I open my mouth to say something about the rising wind, but then I close it again. *Caroline knows what she's doing,* I tell myself—and try very hard to believe it.

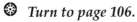 *Turn to page 106.*

I decide to go for the easy job. "Why don't we stay inside and keep your grandmother company?" I say to Caroline.

Mrs. Livingston smiles. "You're a thoughtful girl. Caroline, will you fetch the sewing basket?"

Caroline beams. "Of course!" she exclaims, and hurries from the room.

Then Mrs. Livingston looks at me. "Well, child. Caroline and I have been making nightshirts for injured soldiers and sailors. If a man gets wounded in the chest or arms, the surgeon must tear away his shirt to tend the wound. Sometimes the men are left with nothing but a sheet to cover themselves while they heal."

Uh-oh. I can tell she expects me to help sew shirts, and that sounds complicated. In school last year everyone made a quilt square, and my teacher sewed them together to make a quilt for the principal, who was getting married. Although I sewed my square, I didn't learn how to do anything but straight seams.

I hesitate. On the one hand, I've never sewed clothes before. On the other hand, it would be pretty

cool to leave 1812 knowing that some wounded sailor would end up wearing a shirt that *I* helped make.

 *To help sew,*
   turn to page 103.

 *To find something else to do,*
   turn to page 126.

A sailor appears from behind the blankets with a heavy-looking sack in his hands. "Zeke, *there* you are!" he cries. He tosses the sack to the powder monkey.

"He doesn't seem angry," Caroline whispers to Zeke and me. "Just relieved."

Part of me wants to protect Zeke and keep him away from that gunpowder. *But this is 1812, and he needs this job,* I remind myself. I figure the best thing I can do for Zeke is get him back to work. "Go on, now," I tell him.

Zeke doesn't need any more encouragement, though. He quickly stashes the sack in a leather box and tucks the box under his arm. I guess the box protects the gunpowder while he carries it to the gun crew.

"Good luck!" I say.

"*Thank* you," Zeke answers. Then he races away.

I look at my friend. "I think we just did a good thing."

Another sailor thunders past. Caroline and I squeeze against the wall. "Let's go back to that little kitchen, where we're out of the way," I say.

Caroline leads me back. We find a quiet corner behind some barrels and settle down. Shoulder to shoulder, we listen to the battle going on above our heads. I send up a little prayer that Zeke will be OK.

And all the rest of us too, I add, wondering if a cannonball is going to sink our ship, or if the powder will explode. When an extra-loud crash comes right overhead, Caroline clutches my hand and holds on tight.

Finally the firing stops. The sound of men cheering drifts below deck. Caroline jerks up straight. "They must have done it!" she squeals. "Our men must have captured that British ship!"

As Caroline and I scramble to our feet, Lieutenant Woolsey bursts around a corner and spots us. He stops cold and says, "Thank the good Lord. Miss Caroline! Are you and your friend all right?"

"We're *fine*," she assures him, "as long as you tell me that we won the day."

Lieutenant Woolsey's serious *I'm-an-officer* face splits into a big smile. "We did indeed."

That news makes a lump rise in my throat. Even though I spent the whole fight hiding behind a barrel

like a scared chipmunk, I was *here.* Caroline and I encouraged Zeke right when he needed it most. And I helped Caroline do something for her papa.

"Miss Caroline, I know our success doesn't make up for the British stealing your father's sloop," Lieutenant Woolsey is saying. "Or for your father being taken prisoner. But I hope it helps."

"Oh, it does," she tells him. "It truly does." She looks away for a moment, as if she's trying to collect her thoughts. Then she says, "I know Papa is still a prisoner. And I know the war is a long way from over. But . . ."

Lieutenant Woolsey puts a hand on her shoulder. "Today, we made a difference."

Caroline's face glows. "Yes, sir. We surely did."

✸ *Turn to page 123.*

aroline and I go out to the garden, which is a lot bigger than Mom's flower beds. The carrots and beans and squash are planted in straight rows, so the weeds in between are easy to spot.

After a while my fingers hurt and my back aches, so I'm kind of relieved when rain sprinkles from the clouds. Caroline and I dash inside just as the sprinkle turns into a downpour.

We help Mrs. Livingston cook supper, and soon Caroline's mother comes home from the shipyard. "Is there any news from Lieutenant Woolsey?" Caroline asks at once. "Did the British ship get away?"

"I'm afraid it did," Mrs. Abbott says.

I sink down on a bench. "Oh *no*." I wonder if the few moments it took to get Caroline and me off the navy ship made a difference.

Caroline looks at me with dismay, and I know she's wondering the same thing. Should we have stayed on board? The truth is, we'll never know.

"Now, don't despair," Mrs. Abbott says firmly. "You did show Lieutenant Woolsey the hidden cove. He'll use it to capture a British ship another day."

"Perhaps," Caroline says.

I can tell she's trying not to sound discouraged. "I'm *sure* he will," I tell her. "Even I could see what a good hiding spot it is."

Caroline's mother gives me a smile, like she's pleased with me. "Yes indeed," she says. "Now, girls, let's have our meal."

❋ *Turn to page 118.*

I 'd like to help," I tell Mrs. Livingston, as Caroline returns carrying a big basket piled with pieces of cloth. If Caroline can sew nightshirts, surely I can too.

"Have you assembled clothing before?" Grandmother asks.

"No," I admit.

She nods. "I'll set you to hemming, then. We've got several shirts complete but for the hems."

The nightshirts look sort of like nightgowns for guys. I copy Caroline as she threads her needle, makes a knot, and starts to stitch. But hemming is a whole lot harder than I expected! The linen cloth is stiffer and thicker than the fabric we used in school, so it's hard to push the needle through, and my stitches are too big. They're also crooked, because instead of having lines drawn on the fabric, I've got to just eyeball everything. The thread tangles. My fingers sweat so that it's hard to hold the needle.

After a few minutes of struggling, I end up poking my pinkie. "Ouch!" I cry crossly. I stick my finger in my mouth.

Caroline looks at my stitches with surprise. "Have

you never learned to hem?" she asks. "I love to sew. I'd be glad to help you."

"Thanks," I say through gritted teeth. I take one more stitch, and the thread somehow knots. I use scissors to snip out the knot—and cut into the cloth by mistake.

My heart sinks. I've ruined the nightshirt!

I look at Caroline's grandmother. "I'm very sorry," I tell her, trying not to cry. "I've spoiled this shirt."

"Nonsense!" she says briskly. She takes the shirt from me and spreads it on the table. "Just stitch this little slit back up again. The poor boy who ends up wearing this shirt will likely never notice a small repair. If he does, I imagine he'll be doubly grateful to the girl who worked so hard to help a stranger." She smooths over my rough stitching with a finger. "And your stitches will get more even with practice."

"Thank you, ma'am," I whisper. "I do want to keep trying."

Mrs. Livingston leans over and waits until I look her in the eye. "Failure comes only from giving up," she tells me. "Don't ever scold yourself for trying. Do your best, and all will work out in the end."

Caroline gives me a sideways smile. I smile too. "Yes ma'am," I say. "I'll just keep trying." I check my finger to make sure the bleeding has stopped. Then I get back to work and don't quit until the hem is done.

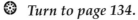 *Turn to page 134.*

L ean to the right, will you? I want to sail around that point." Caroline waves at a long finger of wooded land that juts into the lake. "Isn't it fine to be out? My papa and I used to sail together all the time. Nothing makes us happier than being on the water."

Seeing the joy in Caroline's face as she remembers makes me wish I could tell her about a special memory like that. I think about all the times Mom's tried to talk me into taking more swimming lessons. She swims every day, but I quit after getting through the Guppy class. Once I knew how to keep myself afloat, I didn't see any reason to keep learning new strokes and stuff. Now I'm sorry I didn't try harder to get comfortable doing something Mom loves so much. Maybe I would have enjoyed sharing that with her, the way Caroline shared sailing with her father.

"It's—um—nice to be on the water," I make myself say.

She grins. "Thanks for coming along. I'm not allowed to take the skiff out by myself, and everyone else is almost always too busy to come with me."

As we approach the point, I can't see anything but lake and forest—no people, no boats, no houses or

cabins on shore. Where I live, I'm never too far from other people. Being so alone now is a little spooky— but also kind of cool.

The wind keeps getting stronger, though, and those dark clouds I saw earlier are sailing over the sun. Caroline squints at the sky. "Just a few more minutes, and then we'll turn back," she tells me. "I think a storm is coming, but we have plenty of time to get back to the harbor before it hits." Suddenly she gasps. *"Gracious!"*

We've just rounded the point, and there's a ship up ahead. "Is that . . ." I begin, but my mouth is so dry that it's hard to get the question out.

"Yes," she says, as if she knows exactly what I'm trying to say. "See the flag? That's a British ship!"

My heart starts thumping. "What's a British ship doing *here*?"

Caroline looks from the enemy to the dark gathering clouds and back again. "I suspect the captain hopes to capture a smaller American ship."

"Then shouldn't we get back to Sackets Harbor and tell the navy men?" I ask.

Caroline just stares at the enemy ship with narrowed eyes. "I think it might be better to follow that

schooner. Maybe the British have a hidden cove of their own where they plan to lay a trap for one of *our* ships. If they do, I can tell Lieutenant Woolsey. Otherwise they'll capture another American ship and take another captain prisoner—just like my papa!"

"Wouldn't it be dangerous to chase them?" I ask.

Caroline bites her lower lip. "I don't think they'd fire on a little skiff with just two girls in it," she says slowly.

"You don't *think* the British will fire on us?" I break out in goose bumps. I can't tell if they're from the rising wind or Caroline's plan.

"Well, how can I be sure *what* the blasted British are going to do?" Caroline's eyes glisten with tears.

I'm pretty sure that Caroline knows we should report the British ship, but her heart wants to keep someone else's papa from being captured.

❀ *To report the enemy ship,*
   turn to page 114.

❀ *To follow the enemy ship,*
   turn to page 154.

C aroline and I watch him. We're still in the woods, and Jed doesn't look up, so he doesn't notice us as he passes by.

I whisper, "Isn't that Jed? The woodworker who was sort of rude to you this morning?"

She nods. "When Papa got captured, Jed was the only one who seemed to think that Mama and I couldn't handle things at Abbott's." She crosses her arms and sniffs, clearly still annoyed.

I watch Jed's retreating back. The ax-like thing in his hand looks sharp. "What is he carrying?"

"An adze, for trimming planks." Caroline looks even more annoyed. "Jed may be taking his lunch break, but there's no reason he should have taken that adze from the shipyard. What if someone needs it?"

"Do you think Jed is stealing the adze?" I ask.

"Stealing it?" Caroline repeats, as if that hadn't occurred to her. "That would be awful! Tools are hard to replace." Suddenly she stares at me with horror. "If Jed is stealing tools, our men might not be able to finish the gunboat they're building. And the navy needs that gunboat to fight the British!"

I glare after Jed. I just don't trust that guy!

"The British might even be paying him to make trouble at the shipyard," Caroline adds. "We should run to the shipyard as fast as we can and report what we saw." Then she sucks in her lower lip. "But—if we don't follow Jed right now, we'll never know for certain what he's up to."

"*I* think he's up to no good," I tell Caroline. "We need to follow him."

Caroline doesn't give me time to change my mind. "Quickly, then!" she says in a low tone. "If we stay up here on the forest path, we can see him walking on the beach without him seeing us."

We hurry back along the trail the way we came. We lose sight of Jed once or twice, but we're able to spot him again. We haven't gone far before Caroline puts a hand up to stop me. "I think he's coming into the woods!"

If this guy is working for the British, I don't want him to see us. My skin feels all prickly as I look around for a hiding place. I spot a tree that fell over so long ago that vines have grown up over it. I grab Caroline's hand, and we make our way to the fallen tree. We crouch down behind it just in time. Branches snap as

Jed makes his way into the woods. He's not walking on any path.

Maybe he wants to hide the adze where no one ever goes. If he steals tools one at a time, it might take the shipbuilders a while to figure out what's going on.

Jed's footsteps stop. For a moment the only sound in the forest is a bird singing. Caroline and I look at each other, waiting for something to happen.

"*Yah!*" Jed yells suddenly.

Caroline and I both jump. I can hear somebody's heart beating, but I can't tell if it's hers or mine.

"*Yah!*" Jed hollers again. Then comes a mighty *thump.* He's not trying to hide the adze and creep away again, that's for sure. But what *is* he doing?

❀ *Turn to page 136.*

ery well," Captain Miller tells Caroline and me. He whirls around and shouts, "Men! It's time to leave."

Caroline looks at me, her eyes sparkling with excitement. "Now the men won't have to worry about the skiffs while they take the fort."

Take the fort. I can't believe how easily Caroline says that! I look away, thinking hard. What if Captain Miller is mistaken about the number of British soldiers over there? What if he and his tiny band of "soldiers" don't succeed? Will they get captured? Will Caroline and I get captured too?

Panic bubbles up inside. *Stay calm,* I order myself.

The men start scrambling into the skiffs. I stick close to Caroline, and I'm glad when Seth gets into our boat too. Another man climbs in after him.

Seth rows us away from shore, and then Caroline takes charge and raises the sail. "We've a fair wind today," she says. She sounds totally calm. I can't tell if she's just acting that way to reassure the farmer-soldier or if she really is confident that all will go well.

It doesn't take very long to sail to Pine Island's marshy shore. I stare into the thick woods on land

and shiver. Could a British soldier be watching us right now?

My fear must show, because Seth whispers, "Don't worry. The fort's in a clearing on the far side of the island."

But Caroline leans over and nudges me with her shoulder. I can tell she's thinking the same thing I am: *we're in enemy territory now!*

 Turn to page 121.

Caroline, it's too dangerous to chase a warship. We have to go back to the shipyard and report it right now," I say firmly.

Caroline hesitates, squinting at the British ship and blinking back tears. At last she nods. "You're right," she says reluctantly. "At least with this wind we'll get back to the shipyard in no time."

We head toward Sackets Harbor. The skiff seems to race over the water. I hang on tight.

When we approach Abbott's Shipyard, Mr. Tate comes down the dock to meet us. "Good thing you're back, miss," he calls. "That wind—"

"We spotted an enemy ship!" Caroline hollers, pointing back the way we'd come. "A schooner, heading southwest!"

Mr. Tate takes off like a rocket.

"He'll get word to the navy men," Caroline says, working the oars so that the skiff glides right up to the dock with only a little tiny bump. She sets the oars and ties the skiff to the dock using a fancy knot. But instead of being proud of how well she handles the skiff, she looks frustrated. She may have agreed that we needed to come back to the shipyard, but I can tell

that a big part of her wishes we hadn't.

In fact, her attitude reminds me of how I feel about my mom going away. I know she has to report for duty when the navy tells her to. Am I ready to admit that my mom is doing the right thing, even though it's hard? I sure hope so.

"Caroline," I call. "I know you didn't want to come back here, but we made a good choice."

She pauses, one hand on the ladder. "I'll always wonder if we should have chased after that ship. We might have learned something—something *important*—if only we'd gone a little farther."

"You did the right thing," I insist. I think about my parents, who talk a lot about responsibility. It takes guts to do the responsible thing when your heart wants something else.

Caroline scrambles up the ladder to the dock. "Are you coming?" she calls over her shoulder. "It's almost time for dinner."

I hurry after her. "Caroline, wait," I say.

She turns around. When she sees me, her eyebrows rise. I guess she can tell I've got something on my mind.

"The thing is," I begin, then stop. It's hard to find the right words. "Well . . . I haven't been very responsible lately, or brave either. But after spending time with you, I think I can do better. At least a little."

She's obviously still confused, but she gives me an encouraging nod.

"I'm looking forward to having dinner at your house," I continue. "But afterward, I think I'd better be on my way."

"So soon?" she cries. "I was *so* looking forward to having you stay with me."

I look her straight in the eye. "We'll always be friends, even if we're not together," I promise.

Just like Mom will still be my mom, even when we're far apart. I wish I knew how to tell Caroline about my mom. But of course I can't. How can I explain that I traveled through time?

Suddenly Caroline catches her breath. *"Look!"* She points out over the lake. In the distance, the faint curve of a rainbow is arching over the water, right where a shaft of sunlight slants down through the clouds. "The rain must have started already out there."

"My mother says that rainbows are good omens," I tell her.

Caroline smiles. "My grandmother says that rainbows remind us that life brings rain and sunshine to everyone."

I look at the arc of wavery colors in the sky. Deep inside I know that no matter what, there are going to be some sad times while Mom's gone to sea. But I'm starting to think I just might be able to see those hard days through.

"You know what, Caroline?" I say. "I think everything is going to be all right—for *both* of us."

≥ *The End* ≤

To read this story another way and see how different choices lead to a different ending, go back to page 108.

B y now the kitchen is steamy-hot. The air smells of baking bread, steaming fish, tangy vinegar, and something else I can't figure out. I help Caroline set the table while Mrs. Livingston dishes up the soup we made from boiled whitefish. I've never had fish soup before, but it looks good.

When everything is ready, the four of us settle down at the table. Caroline's black cat, Inkpot, curls up by the fireplace, looking very content. I think he must like hearing everyone's voices and knowing that his family—at least everyone but Mr. Abbott—is together.

"You had a long day at the shipyard, Mrs. Abbott," I say. I'm trying to be part of the conversation without getting into trouble by saying something dumb.

"We've all been working long hours," she explains. "The navy needs a new gunboat as fast as we can build it."

"Our workers will get the job done," Caroline says proudly.

I spread some butter on a thick slice of fresh bread. The bottom is hard and a tiny bit ashy from sitting right on the floor of the bake oven. I swipe the crust with one finger before trying a bite. It is delicious!

If this is what comes from baking bread in a brick oven, I'm all for it.

When the meal is over, Mrs. Abbott fetches some knitting and Caroline and I clear the table. I notice that one kettle is still hanging over the fire. I figure it's dishwater, but when I peek inside, I see thick, dark-gray liquid. It smells kind of metallic and definitely does not look tasty. "Mrs. Livingston, what is this?" I ask.

"I'm melting lead," she says. She waves her hand at a funny-looking gizmo on a nearby shelf. "I got my bullet mold out this morning—"

I gasp. "You're going to make *bullets*?"

"I am indeed," Mrs. Livingston says with a satisfied nod. "Will you hand me the mold?"

I gingerly pick up the bullet mold, which consists of two heavy metal rectangles connected by a hinge. Two wooden handles are on the ends.

"My grandfather was a Patriot who died during the War of Independence," Caroline tells me.

"I wanted to disguise myself as a lad and march off to war with him back in 1776," Mrs. Livingston says. "He wouldn't permit it, though."

"Sometimes I wish *I* could disguise myself as a

lad," Caroline mumbles. She looks frustrated.

"Fetch the ladle, Caroline," Mrs. Livingston says, ignoring her granddaughter's grumbling. "I'm ready to pour the melted lead into the mold." To me she says, "I haven't made bullets for many years, but I still remember how. Some say you can melt down pewter, but in truth, that metal isn't heavy enough. We had a few lead pieces in the storeroom—they used to cover the ridgeline on the roof." She peeks into the kettle and shoves a small log into the fire. "Making bullets is something I can do to help win this war," she adds.

I think about Mom, and how determined *she* is to serve our country. She told me once that she felt privileged to join the navy. I wonder about the first women—whoever they were—to enlist in the U.S. Navy. I bet they had to work extra hard to prove they belonged there. I guess Mom's lucky, in a way. She didn't have to fight for the *opportunity* to serve . . . and if I choose to join the navy one day, I won't either.

❀ *Turn to page 138.*

The two skiffs slow down and ease into the marsh. After Caroline drops the sail, Seth rows us as close to land as possible. I almost shriek with alarm when two ducks explode from the water, *quack-quacking*.

We stop among cattails and other tall water grasses. I can see that this is a good place for Caroline and me to wait out of sight. Seth and the rest of the raiding party slip over the skiffs' sides into mucky water up to their knees. Captain Miller gives Seth and the little boy coils of rope to carry. The men carry guns, which they're careful to keep dry.

"You girls stay right here until we return," the captain orders us in a low but fierce tone. "Is that understood?"

"Yes, sir," Caroline whispers solemnly, and I nod.

"Remember," he adds, "we might need to get away from the island in a hurry."

Caroline grabs a big handful of marsh grass and holds on. "So we don't float away," she murmurs to me. "Can you hang on to the other skiff?"

The second boat is already still, wedged against a big clump of cattails, but I grab the side so it can't possibly float away.

The men wade to shore with barely more than little splishy sounds. Peeking through the cattails, Caroline and I watch them slip into the forest and disappear.

"How long will the raid take?" I whisper.

"I don't know," Caroline whispers back. "When it starts, I expect we'll hear muskets firing. After that, we'll just have to wait."

I'm really bad at waiting. It's so hard to not know what's going on! I find myself fidgeting on the seat. Time seems to pass very, *very* slowly.

Suddenly I hear splashes not far from our hiding spot. It sounds like someone is wading toward us through the marsh. My skin prickles.

Caroline stares at me with wide eyes, and I know we're thinking the same thing: is an enemy soldier sneaking up to capture the skiffs—and us too?

We listen. Silence. *Maybe we were imagining things,* I think hopefully.

Splash!

My hopes sink. That one was even closer! I hold my breath.

✸ *Turn to page 141.*

L ieutenant Woolsey says, "You girls might as well stay here for the present. Once we've secured the British ship, we'll head back to Sackets Harbor."

When he's gone, I grin at Caroline. "Your father is sure going to be proud of you when he gets home!"

Her eyes sparkle with excitement. It's obvious that she can't *wait* to tell her dad how we helped Zeke do his duty during the battle.

That makes me think about my own dad, and what it'll be like for him after Mom leaves. My parents pretty much split cooking and cleaning, but now he's going to be responsible for all of it. And the two of them go out to dinner or a movie together every Wednesday evening. They call it "date night." I realize Dad's not just going to have a lot more to do. He's going to be lonely.

It's kind of strange to think about encouraging my dad, but . . . maybe I'll ask if he and I can go out on Wednesdays now. He'll need a break, and it would be fun to have a chance to talk, just the two of us.

And what about the twins? Mom's the one who makes up silly stories for Britney in the middle of the night if she has a bad dream. And when Sasha paints

a picture, Mom's the one who can always tell what it's supposed to be. Even if it just looks like squiggles.

Once Mom ships out, I'll leave my bedroom door open at night so I can hear Britney if she cries. I'm pretty sure I can make up funny stories that will help her forget her nightmares. And I bet Sasha will love it if I paint *with* her.

I promise myself to give it all a try. I'm really grateful that my sisters and I don't have to worry about making our way alone, like Zeke does.

I turn to Caroline. "When we get back to the village, I need to go," I tell her.

"So soon?" she protests. "I wish you could stay. After what's happened, my family and friends will want to have a celebration dinner tonight!"

"That would be nice," I say honestly. "But I sort of want to find my own family now."

Caroline nods. I can tell that she understands. "I can walk with you a little way," she offers.

"No, thank you," I say. My eyes feel a little teary at the thought of leaving her, but I manage to smile. This is *her* time, and *her* place. I need to go back to my own.

Before long we're back on dry land. Caroline and I exchange hugs, and I walk out of the village. As soon as I'm sure I'm alone, I use the compass to return home.

Once I'm back by the pond, I take the trail to my house. When I reach the backyard, I see my parents and my sisters playing soccer. They don't notice me for a few minutes. Then Mom glances in my direction and walks over to join me.

I've got something important to say, so I talk fast. "Mom, I know the work you do in the navy is really important. And I know you're going to do a wonderful job while you're off on your ship."

Mom looks startled. Then her eyes get shiny, as if she's about to cry. "Oh, sweetie," she says. "Thank you for saying those things."

"I'll do my best to keep Dad's spirits up," I promise. "And the twins' spirits, too." After all, it might just make a big difference.

≥ The End ≤

To read this story another way and see how different choices lead to a different ending, go back to page 53.

"I 'd better not do any sewing," I say reluctantly. "I don't really know how to make clothes."

"As you wish," Caroline's grandmother says.

I sit on the bench beside the kitchen table, watching Caroline and Mrs. Livingston settle in to sew. It's totally boring. Watching Caroline's needle flash in and out so skillfully also makes me jealous, which is not a good feeling.

Maybe I should try to help, I think. But I can tell that Caroline and Mrs. Livingston are really good at sewing. These nightshirts are important, and I'd just mess one up if I tried.

Then I notice that there are some dirty dishes sitting on a small table across the room. "Um . . . pardon me," I say hesitantly. "I'd be happy to wash those dishes for you. If that's all right, I mean."

Mrs. Livingston nods approvingly. "That would be kind," she says.

"We've a well by the back garden," Caroline adds.

It takes a long time to figure out how to get water out of the well, but I don't want to let Caroline and her grandmother know that I don't know how to do this either. I have to lower a heavy wooden bucket

down into the well with a rope and then haul it back up again. The full bucket is so heavy that I can hardly manage, and some water slops out while I'm hauling it. In the kitchen, I pour the water into a kettle that hangs in the fireplace and build up a fire beneath it. (Thank goodness I've gone camping and at least know how to build a fire.) Then I wait until the water gets warm. At this rate, it would take another hour for the water to get really hot.

"There's some soap in the crock there on the mantel," Mrs. Livingston says.

I find the soap, which looks homemade, and scrape bits into the kettle. I lug more water inside to rinse the dishes after they're washed. Caroline tells me to haul the dirty water outside and pour it carefully over plants in the garden.

When I'm finally finished I think, *I know one thing for sure: I will never complain again about having to fill or empty the dishwasher.* I remember how I yelled at Mom this morning when she asked me to do something that would have taken about one minute, and my face gets hot. I really do need to stop feeling sorry for myself.

"Thank you for washing up," Caroline tells me.

"With Papa gone and Mama so busy at the shipyard, sometimes I feel as if chores never end. I wish I could spend all my time doing things to help win the war and get Papa back."

"You help more than you know," her grandmother says. "Every time you do extra chores, you let me spend more time making bandages or nightshirts or even bullets for the soldiers and sailors. Every time you're cheerful about what you can do, instead of complaining about what you can't do, you give your mother one less thing to worry about."

I look out the window, thinking about my own mom. I haven't been making it any easier for her to report for duty on her ship. I guess I should stop whining and give her one less thing to worry about. And what about Dad? If I do my chores without complaining while Mom's gone, and maybe even look for extra ways to help, I'll be giving him one less thing to worry about, too.

❀ *Turn to page 134.*

W e wait for another sailor to run past before crawling as quickly as we can toward the wounded man. My knees get all tangled up in my skirt and petticoat, so I grab a handful of cloth and jerk as hard as I can. The fabric makes a *ri-i-i-ip* sound, and all of a sudden it's easier to move.

We reach the hurt sailor. He has long coppery hair and looks like he should be in high school, not on this ship. His face has gone so white that his freckles stand out like tiny drops of brown ink. He's sort of panting—short breaths in and out—so I know his shoulder must really hurt. Blood is squeezing through his fingers where he's clutching the wound.

Another thunderous cannon shot makes the air tremble. Drifting smoke stings my nose and throat and eyes. What if the very next cannonball is the one that sinks our ship?

Think about being helpful, I order myself, *instead of freaking out.* My Girl Scout troop has practiced first aid, and I try to remember what we learned. But Caroline and I don't even have a first aid kit! No bandages, no *nothing.* I sure wish my parents were here. They would know what to do.

Then Caroline gets to the point. "Sir?" she asks kindly. "How can we help?"

The wounded young man seems to notice us for the first time. "I—I don't think I'm hurt bad," he tells us. "But I'm done for if I don't get the bleeding stopped. If you could just press some cloth or something on the wound—"

"Of course!" I exclaim, because now I remember two things: what I learned about putting pressure on a wound, and the fact that I've already made a long rip in my skirt. I grab the dangling piece and yank again. Once I have a wad of loose cloth in my hands, I cover the gash in his shoulder and push down with gentle but steady pressure.

"It feels better already," the sailor says. "Thank you."

"That's clever thinking," Caroline whispers to me.

I feel a flush of pride. "I'm just glad I can help," I whisper back.

"My grandmother would approve," she adds. "Whenever I complain about something, she just says, 'Well, what are you going to do about it?'"

"Your grandmother sounds like a smart lady." I manage a tiny smile.

With another piece of my skirt, I tie the bandage in place. Applying basic first aid won't win the war for the Americans, but it makes a difference to *this* guy. That's enough to make me feel pretty good.

A moment later, though, I see blood seeping through the bandage. This time I stay calm. "Tear another piece of cloth from my skirt," I tell Caroline. "It's ruined anyway."

She does as I ask. I fold the fabric and gently press it over the man's bandage. "I'll hold this in place," I tell him. "Try not to move your arm."

"I—I thank you, miss," he murmurs. He closes his eyes. Maybe he's lost so much blood already that he's feeling woozy.

There's nothing more we can do but wait for help. "I sure hope this battle ends soon," I whisper to Caroline.

She nods. "I do too." She hesitates before adding, "I'm truly sorry that I insisted we stay on board for the chase. I just got so excited!"

"Don't feel bad," I tell her. "I agreed to come along. And the thing is . . ." I stop, trying to find words to explain the idea that's taking shape in my mind. "Once

the cannonballs started flying, I told myself I must have been insane for agreeing to stay on board. But now—well, now I know that something *good* happened because we stayed." I glance at the hurt sailor. "I guess once you've made a decision, you just have to trust yourself and do the best you can, no matter *what* happens next."

Caroline thinks for a moment, then nods. I can tell that she understands what I mean. If we'd left the ship, this guy might have bled to death before anyone had time to tend him.

It seems as if the cannon booms go on forever. Then all of a sudden the shooting stops, and the men on deck start cheering. "The British are lowering their flag!" a sailor shouts.

"We've won the day!" Caroline exclaims. "That British ship is ours!" Tears glisten in her eyes. I know she's thinking of her papa's ship—the one the British stole.

"I'm glad you got to see this," I tell her. She smiles and nods, as if her heart is so full and overflowing that she can't even find words.

I don't want to ruin this victory moment, so I don't say anything more. Once the wounded sailor is taken

care of and Caroline and I get back to shore, though, I'll tell her it's time for me to leave.

I want to ask my dad if I can volunteer at the hospital where he works. Or maybe I can volunteer in a veterans' hospital. I'd feel good about helping sick or wounded patients, and staying busy will keep me from worrying about Mom.

I know a girl in my own time won't be allowed to help with medical stuff—and that's fine by me! But when I think about that sailor with the copper-colored hair, what I'll always remember is the look of gratitude in his eyes. At a moment when he must have felt terribly alone, Caroline and I showed up to help.

➤ *The End* ➤

To read this story another way and see how different choices lead to a different ending, go back to page 38.

C aroline folds a finished nightshirt and places it in a basket with several others. I start to wonder about the hospital where these shirts will end up. I've visited the hospital where my dad works, so I'm kind of curious to see what an 1812 hospital is like. I wouldn't want to visit right after a battle or something—no *way*. But today the hospital should be pretty quiet.

"I don't know if this would be all right," I say hesitantly. "But I was wondering if we might deliver the nightshirts."

Caroline sits up straight. I can tell she likes my idea.

"That would be fine," Mrs. Livingston declares. "We've got several complete, and they're not doing any good sitting here. Just take shawls along, in case the rain moves in."

"We'll be back in time to help with supper," Caroline promises. Then she grabs the basket and grins at me. "Let's go!"

Caroline leads me back through Sackets Harbor. We're close to the water when she stops suddenly. "I thought of something," she says. "A widow lady in town just opened a new inn that's not far from here. She serves food and has a couple of bedrooms for

travelers. It's small, but with so many people crowding into town, I'm sure she's very busy. Since you need to find work, shall we stop and see if she needs help?"

 To visit the inn,
    go online to beforever.com/endings.

 To continue on to the hospital,
    turn to page 156.

B eside me, Caroline lifts her head very, very slowly. I hold my breath and find a little peep-hole through the vines.

Jed stands not too far away. He's panting, his shoulders heaving up and down. "This is what you deserve!" he yells, swinging the adze like some major-league baseball player hitting a home run. The adze blade slams into a tree, and a chunk of wood goes flying. Who is he talking to?

"He's going to break our adze!" Caroline whispers indignantly. "I have to stop him!"

"Caroline, no!" I hiss. "It's too dangerous!" She's already scrambling to her feet. I try to grab her arm, but she's too quick for me.

She crashes out of our hiding spot. "Stop that!" she cries.

Jed whirls around with a look of alarm. When he sees Caroline, alarm turns into anger. "What are you doing here?" he demands.

I scramble to my feet too. "Don't you hurt Caroline!" I holler.

Jed looks from her to me and back again. "I'm not going to hurt Miss Caroline," he says, like I've said

something crazy. He lets the adze dangle in his hand. "I can explain."

Caroline hesitates. Then she crosses her arms and lifts her chin. "We saw you trying to break that adze, Jed. How can you explain *that*?"

✸ *Turn to page 143.*

aroline's grandmother interrupts my thoughts. "I obeyed my husband during the Revolution. I stayed home and tended the farm and made bullets and knit warm socks, while he fought and died."

Mrs. Abbott looks up from her knitting. "And when the War for Independence was won thirty years ago, you surely didn't expect to be fighting the British again."

"That's right. You beat them fair and square!" I add.

"Well, they're back," Mrs. Livingston says flatly, "so we must do what we can to help run them off—for good, this time." She gives Caroline a meaningful look. "We can still find ways to be useful, even if we can't march off to war."

I really, really, *really* want to say that one day, women *will* be able to serve in the military. The words almost burst out of me! I want to tell my new friends that my mom is in the navy, and that I'm proud of her. But I don't quite dare.

Then I look at Caroline and her mom and grandmother. If I didn't think it would sound dumb, I'd say I'm proud of *them*. It's pretty cool how each one is doing

her best to help America win the war. I bet my female ancestors were strong and capable during the war, just like them!

Caroline and I watch as Mrs. Livingston ladles the steaming gray liquid into the mold. She won't let us help, because if our hands shook we might spatter the hot lead. "Now, I need to let the bullets cool," she says. "They'll harden right up."

Then she looks from me to Caroline and back again. Her eyes start to twinkle. "I have a surprise," she says. "The oven was still hot when I took the bread out, so while you girls weeded the garden, I baked small cakes."

"Ooh!" Caroline bounces on her toes. "Thank you, Grandmother. What a treat."

I'm not sure what small cakes are, but I soon discover that they're basically cookies. Mrs. Livingston's cookies have cinnamon in them. In fact, they taste a lot like the snickerdoodles my mom and I make! "These are wonderful," I say, nibbling my cookie slowly to make it last. "Thank you, Mrs. Livingston."

"Mama?" Caroline asks. "Would you like one?"

Mrs. Abbott smiles. "Yes indeed." When Caroline

brings over the plate, Mrs. Abbott pulls her close for a moment and kisses her cheek.

After our treat, we do the dishes. By that time, the sun is setting. Caroline gives me a hopeful grin. "Would you like to return to the shipyard tomorrow? I know you probably need to look for work, but perhaps we could have one more day of fun. *Please?*"

❀ *Turn to page 148.*

I peek through the cattails. Up ahead, tall grasses whip back and forth like somebody's thrashing around, and we hear the biggest splash yet. "Oh!" someone cries. The voice is high-pitched. I feel a little relief—at least it must be a *young* British soldier. Then I realize he'll still be carrying a gun.

It's hard not to panic. If I'm captured, will I have a chance to use my compass to get home? I decide it doesn't matter, because I couldn't leave Caroline as a prisoner all by herself. I just *couldn't*.

Then some tall reeds part up ahead, and I catch sight of the wader. I can hardly believe my eyes. It's no soldier—it's a girl! She's about our own age, wearing a white cap and a faded green dress covered with mud. The girl stares at us, obviously shocked.

"Who are you?" Caroline demands.

"Who are *you*?" she asks in turn. She takes a step backward, loses her footing in the mud, and struggles to stay upright.

This girl is in such a bad spot that it's impossible to be afraid of her. "We asked first," I say.

"Very well," she answers in a low voice. "My name is Martha. My mother's a laundress for the soldiers at

the fort, and I help her." Her eyes glisten with tears. "I was hanging out sheets when your men came. I saw what was happening, so I ran away. I thought I might hide here."

"Oh," I say. My voice sounds kind of puny. It had never occurred to me that there might be women or girls at the fort. What are we supposed to do *now*?

⚙ *Turn to page 146.*

M iss Caroline, I couldn't break this if I tried all day." Jed holds up the adze. "I just needed something to practice with."

I edge closer. "Practice?" I ask. "Practice what?"

"Fighting the British," Jed mutters.

I frown. "You expect us to believe that you'd fight the British with a carpenter's tool?"

Something flashes in his eyes, as if I've hurt his feelings or embarrassed him somehow. "Yes, miss, I do. Everybody says the British could attack Sackets Harbor again at any time. And if they come, it's the ships and tools and such they'll be after."

I still don't get it. "So?"

He turns to Caroline. "There isn't a man at Abbott's who isn't determined to fight the British and defend the shipyard. But most of us don't have anything to fight *with*. Just a couple of the older men have their own muskets. I don't even have a knife."

"O-o-oh," I say slowly.

"Yesterday, the British just shot some cannonballs at us from the lake. But next time, they'll likely come ashore. And the truth is . . . well . . . I've never been in a real fight." Jed stares at his toes. "I decided I'd better be

thinking about what I'll do when the British march into Sackets Harbor. So instead of eating my midday meal, I borrowed this and came out here where nobody would see me, and . . ." His cheeks get red, as if he's ashamed.

I feel a little ashamed too. I sure was quick to think the worst of Jed.

"Oh Jed, I'm sorry I accused you of doing something wrong," Caroline says earnestly. "We didn't mean to spy on you. We just happened to see you walking along the beach—"

"And you did look pretty suspicious," I add, hoping he'll understand.

"Talk to Mr. Tate," Caroline urges Jed. "Explain what you're doing. I suspect he'll be quite proud of you. He may even organize all the men to prepare for a fight! We should have a good plan in place for the day the British come back."

The day the British come back. Not *if* the British come. Caroline knows in her heart that sooner or later, the enemy will attack her village again. It makes me feel sad—but proud, too. I'm proud of people like Caroline and Jed and my great-great-great-whatever-

grandfather. They may not have had proper guns, but they still beat the British.

"We'll leave you to it," Caroline adds to Jed.

He nods.

Caroline and I find the path again and head back toward the village. After a moment we hear Jed yell again, fainter this time, as he gets back to his practice.

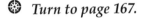 *Turn to page 167.*

B ut . . . what did you intend to do after our men captured all the soldiers?" Caroline asks Martha.

"I *hope* my mother will be left in peace and I can go back to her," Martha says. "She's just a poor widow trying to earn a living. She's told me many times that if Americans attack, I must hide, and then hang a red shirt we've saved from the branch of a tree. A fisherman we know will see it and come take me to safety."

Caroline shifts on the seat so that Martha can't see her face. "Gracious," she whispers to me. "Martha and her mother have been working at the British fort. They might know things about the enemy that our men need to hear. Perhaps we should bring her aboard and hold her until Captain Miller returns." She hesitates. "Then again . . . she's just a young girl."

A young girl, like Caroline and me.

I lean close to Caroline. "If there's any information to get, surely our men can get it from Martha's mother—or from the British soldiers."

Caroline looks torn. "But we don't even know if the raid will be successful."

I look back at Martha, standing in water up to her waist. Maybe *she* can tell us how the raid is going.

"Martha, what exactly did you see back there?" I ask.

Martha wipes a tear from her cheek, leaving a muddy streak. "I saw your men burst through the gate," she says. "We've only four soldiers here at the moment, and they were completely surprised. One of your men grabbed the sentry. Then I ran. That's all I know."

⚙ *To let Martha stay hidden,*
   turn to page 152.

⚙ *To capture Martha,*
   turn to page 162.

I'm really tempted to say yes. I know for sure that any day spent with Caroline Abbott is a day full of excitement! But seeing her with her mom makes me homesick for my own mother. I want to go home soon so I can spend time with her before she ships out.

I think hard about what to say and how to say it. "I'd like to spend the night, if I may, but in the morning I need to travel on."

"Travel on?" Caroline cries. "To where? I was hoping you'd stay in Sackets Harbor!"

"Now, Caroline," Grandmother says softly. "If your guest needs to go, you mustn't urge her to stay. Savor the time you have left with her, instead of worrying about the leaving." She looks at me and nods slowly. Her eyes are so intelligent that I wonder again if somehow she knows there's more to my story than I can tell.

"You're welcome to visit anytime," Mrs. Abbott adds kindly.

"Thank you, ma'am," I say. "Perhaps I will."

I slide my hand into my pocket and squeeze the compass. Maybe I *will* come back again. It will

be easier to leave knowing it won't be forever.

Caroline and I go out to the backyard and use the "privy," which is what they call an outhouse. Then we head up to her bedroom. It's small, but she doesn't have to share it with anybody, and she can see the harbor from her window.

"I have a spare nightgown and cap you can wear," she offers.

"Is it as pretty as yours?" I blurt. Caroline's nightgown is beautifully embroidered.

She smiles as she hands me her spare gown— which *is* just as pretty. "I do like to stitch," she says in an offhand way, as if her delicate work is nothing special.

We start to undress. All of a sudden Caroline says, "I just got a wonderful idea! Shall we exchange hair ribbons? Then we'd each have a memento of your visit."

"I *would* like that," I say. To be honest, I hadn't paid any attention to my hair, but when I borrow Caroline's brush and mirror, I discover that I'm wearing a pale blue ribbon. When I offer it to Caroline, she grins and hands me a pink one. I'm not sure if the pink ribbon

will survive the trip back to my own time, but it's worth a try.

Once we've changed into our nightgowns, we lie down. My head is so full of everything I've seen and done in 1812 that I'm afraid I'll never get to sleep. Caroline must be having trouble too, because she tosses and turns. Finally she whispers, "I wish you didn't have to go. There aren't any girls my own age close by, and it's been so nice having a new friend. I'll miss you."

"I'll miss you too," I say.

Caroline asks, "Shall we always be friends?"

"Always," I agree. "And Caroline? Thank you for giving me a day I'll never forget."

"I'll never forget you," she says. "I admire your courage."

That catches me by surprise. "You're the courageous one!"

"You're traveling all by yourself!" She sits up in bed so that she can look at me in the moonlight. "Next time I feel sorry for myself, I'm going to think about you. Having Papa gone is dreadful, but at least I'm at home, with Mama and Grandmother and Mr. Tate and all the shipyard workers."

I want to tell her that I'm not really traveling by myself, and that I've got a home and people who love me too—but of course I can't explain it. *Besides,* I think, *in a way I **am** traveling by myself.* I traveled back two hundred years in time and did things I would never have dreamed I could do. I guess I *can* dig up some courage when I need to.

⊕ *Turn to page 157.*

I think we should let her stay hidden," I tell Caroline in a low voice.

Caroline gives one short nod. "Yes. Let's leave the poor girl in peace." She looks back at Martha. "Are you sure you'll be all right by yourself?"

Martha lifts her chin. "Quite sure," she says. I can tell she's trying really hard to seem in control. Honestly, though, even with her chin in the air she just looks frightened and miserable.

Without another word, she turns and begins making her way farther into the marsh. She soon disappears into the reeds and cattails. Caroline heaves a big sigh. "Sometimes," she says, "it's simply impossible to know if you're doing the right thing."

"I know," I agree. "I guess we just have to make the best decision we can, and then live with it."

For some reason, an image of Mom pops into my mind. I always figured she just *knew* that joining the navy was the right thing for her, but now I wonder: Was that a hard decision? Did she struggle to choose between staying home with her family and doing what she believes is her patriotic duty? Does she ever have second thoughts? For the first time, I realize that even

if she does, she can't change her decision now.

"Do you suppose parents ever wish they'd done things differently?" I ask Caroline.

She looks startled by the question. For a moment she stares at a turtle sitting motionless on a half-submerged log. Finally she says, "I hope my papa isn't wasting time wishing we hadn't gone sailing the day he was captured. He had no way to know what was going to happen, and regrets won't help anything."

"Right." I wipe a few drops of sweat from my forehead, thinking that over. Mr. Abbott getting captured isn't the same thing as my mom choosing to go away. But in both cases, what's done is done.

I'm sorry, Mom, I think. I've never given her credit for making a tough decision and then making the best of it. When I get back home, I'll try to do better.

≥ *The End* ≤

To read this story another way and see how different choices lead to a different ending, go back to page 147.

Let's go after them," I say. "Just promise we'll stay far enough back that they can't fire on us."

"I promise," Caroline says.

I glance at the sky. The clouds overhead are getting darker, and little waves are rocking the skiff. "And if the weather gets *really* bad, we'll head to shore, right?"

"Right." Caroline's already adjusting the sail. The wind smacks the canvas, and the skiff zooms over the blue-green water toward the British schooner.

Then the skiff lurches, and I have to hang on tight to stay on the seat. "How do you steer this thing?" I ask. We're zigzagging instead of going in a straight line.

"I have to work with the wind," she says without looking at me, because she's really focused on the lake and the schooner. "Sailing is faster than rowing, but it's *almost* too windy now to use the sail . . ." She glances at the canvas, which is stretched taut with the wind. "I don't want to bring it down before I absolutely have to, though. If we switch to the oars, that British schooner will get away for *sure.*"

I need to do something besides sit here like a lump. "Can I help?" I shout over the rising wind.

"Keep your eyes on the schooner!" she yells back.

I try extremely hard, but every now and then an extra-sharp burst of wind hits the sail, and the whole skiff shudders. I bite my tongue to keep from begging to turn back, but finally I can't stand it anymore. "Caroline—"

"It's time to head to shore," she agrees. "I'm going to lower the sail."

The wind blasts my hair away from my face and smacks the sail with a loud cracking sound. Caroline struggles with the rope that runs the sail up and down. Her face is set, and her mouth is clamped in a tight line.

"Caroline?"

She doesn't answer. Her hands clench the rope so hard that her knuckles are white.

She needs help, I think. I may not know anything about sailing, but I can help haul on a rope. I stand up and take a step—

"Sit *down!*" Caroline cries.

The skiff lurches beneath my feet. Another blast of wind knocks into me. Then the whole world tips sideways.

✹ *Turn to page 170.*

I 'm having too much fun doing things with you to think about getting a job now," I say.

That brings a smile to Caroline's face. "I'm having fun too," she says. "Let's be on our way."

We pass the shipyards and walk on toward some long, low buildings. The wood used to build them looks pale and raw. *These buildings must be pretty new,* I think.

Caroline leads me to one of the buildings. "This is the hospital," she says. The door is wide open—no air-conditioning in 1812, I remind myself—so we walk inside.

Two rows of cots are lined up along the walls. Every cot is occupied. The room smells of bad things—I'm not even sure what. Sickness, I guess, and not enough clean clothes and wash water. Some of the patients don't look much older than me. Another one has a long gray beard. One man has a bloodstained bandage wrapped around his forehead.

All of a sudden I feel nervous. Maybe this visit wasn't such a good idea.

❀ *Turn to page 160.*

I sleep on a bed made of quilts and blankets on the floor of Caroline's bedroom. It's as comfortable as a sleeping bag, but I'm wide-awake before the sun rises. I decide to leave now, before Caroline wakes. There's no writing paper in sight, but I spot a little slate—the kind pioneer kids in TV shows use in their one-room schoolhouses. Very carefully I write *Good-bye, Caroline* with the skinny little slate pencil.

I wrap Caroline's pink ribbon around the compass, making sure I can still see the N for north. Then I hold the compass in both hands, slowly turn until the needle points straight away from me, and close my eyes.

Dizziness washes over me, and I wait for it to pass before opening my eyes. I see the familiar pond, the familiar woods . . . and the familiar hummingbird whirring right beside me. *No time has passed while I was in 1812,* I think. After a moment, the beautiful little bird swoops away.

To my delight, the pink ribbon has traveled back with me. I fold it carefully and tuck it into my pocket.

I walk the path through the woods quickly, think-ing about everything that's happened. I'm super-glad

I went to Sackets Harbor. I'm also super-glad to be home.

When I've almost reached my yard, the back door to my house opens. Mom, Dad, and the twins come outside. "Who wants to play soccer?" Dad asks.

"Me! Me!" Britney and Sasha yell. They're too little for real soccer, but they've come to a lot of my games and they like to pretend that they can play.

Mom finds the ball under one of the rosebushes. "Ready?" she calls. She rolls it across the grass, and the twins take off running.

I smile and get a lump in my throat at the same time. I still wish Mom could stay home, playing soccer and baking snickerdoodles and weeding her flower beds when she has time. But when I think about Caroline, staring over the huge lake and missing her papa really, really hard . . . well, I guess being able to connect with Mom by e-mail and Skype is a whole lot better than nothing. And it's good to know that if Mom ever did get hurt, the other doctors on board have modern science to take care of her.

In fact, everything is a whole lot easier than it was two hundred years ago.

It's going to be hard to see Mom leave, I think, but I'd better not waste any more time while she's home.

I walk out of the woods. "Hey," I call. "Can I play too?"

≈ *The End* ≈

To read this story another way and see how different choices lead to a different ending, go back to page 45.

I don't see anybody who looks like a doctor, but a woman sitting beside one of the cots glances up and comes to greet us. She's quite pretty, with a round face and dark brown hair. "May I help you girls?" she asks.

"Do you work here?" I ask doubtfully. I don't think she's a nurse, because she's wearing a yellow dress with lace around the neck.

"I'm visiting my husband while he recovers from a bad fever," she explains.

Caroline holds up the basket. "We brought some new nightshirts, ma'am."

The lady smiles. "Why, they will be greatly appreciated! But your sweet faces will do the men just as much good. Why don't you go and say hello to them?"

I exchange a glance with Caroline. She gives me a *Let's go* nod. We're not having any trouble understanding each other. It feels like we've been friends forever.

Caroline and I walk to the closest cot, where a man who looks about my dad's age is sitting up, propped against the wall. His left hand is totally wrapped up in a bandage.

"Who have we here?" he asks with a friendly smile. "I'm mighty glad to see you. I've been ever so bored."

We introduce ourselves. "Are you in need of a nightshirt?" I ask.

"No, thank you, I'm fine," he tells us. "Now that lad over there—the one with the sheet pulled up to his chin? He's in need. But please—will one of you do something for me?"

Caroline and I exchange another look. "Why don't I give these out," she tells me, holding up the basket.

She goes on her way, and I turn back to the patient. "What can I do for you, sir?" I ask. I can't imagine what the man wants, but I'll help him if I can.

✪ *Turn to page 175.*

I think we should hold on to Martha," I tell Caroline in a low voice. "We need to let Captain Miller decide what to do with her."

Caroline watches a red-winged blackbird hopping along a nearby reed. Finally she says, "I don't want to capture her."

Martha is still standing in the water, looking half proud and half scared. I can hardly meet her gaze. "I don't either," I admit in a whisper. "But . . ."

"But we must," Caroline finishes unhappily. "Oh, I do *hate* this war."

"Well?" Martha calls.

Caroline takes the oars, and we gently glide to Martha. "You must stay with us," Caroline tells her. "You'll be treated fairly, I promise."

Martha hangs her head for a moment. Then she nods. "Very well. Would you be so kind as to help me into your boat?"

It takes both Caroline and me to tug Martha into the skiff. She lands in a heap, caked with black mud and pretty much soaked. But she scrambles onto one of the seats and sits with her back straight. I really admire the way she's handling herself. Something bad

has happened to her, and she's not—as my dad would say—weeping and wailing. And *that* thought makes me feel a little guilty. If Martha can get taken prisoner without whining, surely I can help my dad without whining after Mom leaves.

Caroline takes us back to the other skiff. I can't tell if I feel guilty or proud about our choice. It occurs to me that maybe Caroline and I have been a little bit brave. Taking a soaking girl "prisoner" wasn't frightening, but it was something we really didn't want to do.

Neither one of us says another word after we reach the meeting spot. Martha doesn't speak either. We still haven't heard any muskets firing. A frog makes a *ka-lunk* sound, but otherwise everything is still.

It seems like we wait for a lo-o-ong time. The wind kicks up, and it feels more and more like it might rain. I rest my chin on my hand, wondering if I'm about to get soaked.

Suddenly triumphant shouts ring from the woods. I jerk up straight. Am I hearing British soldiers or the Americans?

Seth bursts from the forest. "Huzzah for the United States!" he shouts joyfully. "We captured the fort with

not a shot fired! Pine Island is now in *American* hands."

"They've done it!" Caroline cries. "They've captured the British fort!"

The American men appear, herding four British soldiers. They don't look scary at all, just sort of bummed out. They seem ready to do whatever they're told.

There is no woman with them. The Americans must have decided to let Martha's mom go free. That makes me very happy. It means Captain Miller will let Martha go, too.

Caroline clutches my hand. "Oh, *thank* you for coming along," she says. Her eyes are shining. "I know that capturing four British soldiers might not seem of much importance, but—"

"It *is* important," I tell her firmly. "Your father will be very proud of you."

I'm pretty amazed that everything turned out so well. What an adventure! I never would have guessed it, but Caroline and I really were able to do something that just might help win the war.

While Caroline and I are grinning at each other, Seth splashes into the marsh. He pulls our skiff up to the beach. He's grinning too.

Caroline introduces Martha to Captain Miller
and explains her situation. "You are free to go, miss,"
he tells Martha. "You'll find your mother waiting
for you at the fort. I did not come here to make war
on women."

"Thank you, sir," Martha says formally. "My mother
is alone in the world, and she needs me." She climbs
from the boat, but before heading into the woods, she
looks at me and Caroline. "And thank you for treating
me with respect."

After Martha leaves, I keep thinking about what
she said. *My mother is alone in the world, and she needs
me.* Once my mom goes to sea, will my dad feel like
he's alone in the world? I've never heard him say one
negative word about my mom being gone, but he must
be dreading it too. Everything they used to do together
will land right on his shoulders. And I haven't given
him any reason to hope that he can count on me to
pitch in.

When I get home, maybe I should spend a little
less time complaining and a little more time trying to
figure out how I can help Dad. Like putting plates in
the dishwasher without being asked, and thinking up

new ways to keep the twins occupied. I know! We can all start making a whole new photo album. The twins love projects like that, and staying busy will help keep them from missing Mom too badly. Besides, if we take pictures of everything that happens while Mom's away, maybe she'll feel like she didn't totally miss it all.

Suddenly, I can hardly wait to get started on that. Once we're back in Sackets Harbor, I'll explain to Caroline that my parents are having a hard time and need me.

The American men settle the prisoners into the two skiffs. When we shove off, I can see that we're riding really low in the water now, but Caroline looks as confident as ever handling the skiff. "I'm about to set sail!" she announces.

I smile. We're heading for the American shore, and for home.

≥ The End ≤

To read this story another way and see how different choices lead to a different ending, go back to page 74.

I 'm so glad I didn't rush back to the shipyard and report my suspicions," Caroline tells me. "Jed might have gotten in trouble. At the least he would have been horribly embarrassed before everything got sorted out. He wouldn't want the men to know he's afraid."

Caroline's words catch me by surprise. I'm afraid of so many things that it still seems surprising that someone who acts so tough, like Jed, might be scared inside. "You know," I say slowly, "maybe Jed's not just afraid of the British. Maybe he's scared of letting your father down or embarrassing himself in front of the men."

Caroline stops walking. "I hadn't thought of it like that."

I watch a gull fly along the lakeshore, thinking how impressed I am with Jed. It's one thing for men like Lieutenant Woolsey to fight the British with cannons and muskets. It's quite another for a barefoot teenager to defend a shipyard with nothing but an adze.

"I bet it helps Jed to know that you think his practice is a good idea," I tell Caroline. "What you said

probably gave him a lot of encouragement." Maybe
Caroline and I did something to help win the war
today after all.

I think of how I acted right before running out of
my house this morning, shouting at Mom and all, and
my cheeks get warm. The memory is embarrassing.
Maybe when I get home I should try to figure out some
way to be encouraging.

We round a bend, and there's Sackets Harbor
in front of us. "Let's head to the house, shall we?"
Caroline says.

I'd like to see Caroline's house, but honestly, my
head is spinning. I feel as if my brain is about to
explode with all the new things I've seen and experi-
ences I've had. I remember thinking I didn't want to
be with my own family, but now, that's *exactly* what
I want.

"Um, Caroline, the thing is . . ." My voice trails
away.

"Oh." She studies me, looking disappointed.
"You've changed your mind about staying with us
for a few days, haven't you."

"I really would like to stay," I say quickly. "But the

thing is . . . I need to continue my journey. I—well,
I want to find my family."

Something kind of fierce flashes in Caroline's eyes.
She throws her arms around me and squeezes me into
a big hug. "That's more important than anything," she
whispers. "I hope you find them quickly."

I pull away and look her in the eye. "And I hope
your father comes home soon," I tell her. "Thank you
for today. I'll never forget you."

She nods, and then turns toward the village. I wait
until she's out of sight before pulling the compass from
my pocket. It's time to go home.

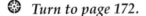 *Turn to page 172.*

I cy water grabs me as I plunge into the lake. When I try to scream, I get a mouthful of water. I thrash around, but it doesn't do any good. I can't see anything but green-blue water. I can't hear anything but muffled thumps that sound very far away. Sinking in this cold, deep water is my worst nightmare. *Mom!* I scream silently. *Dad! Help me!*

But Mom and Dad can't help me. Not here.

Kick toward the surface! I think, but my long skirt and petticoat are all tangled around my legs. I reach down and try to drag the heavy cloth away—and my hand hits a hard lump. The compass! It's still in my pocket, and it can get me safely home. I have to use it.

But—no. Caroline would spend the rest of her life thinking that I'd drowned. I can't do that to her.

OK, I order myself. *For once in your life, just be brave!*

I grab handfuls of my skirt and pull upward, *hard.* Suddenly my legs are free. The water looks lighter above my head, so I keep my gaze fixed in that direction and kick my legs as hard as I can.

Just when I'm sure I can't hold my breath for one more second, my face pops above the water. I gasp and suck in a big gulp of air.

The water is really choppy now. I pump my legs like I'm riding a bicycle, and slap the water with my hands, and I just barely manage to keep my face above the surface. I won't be able to keep this up for long, and I can't see anything but lake.

"Caroline?" I shriek. "Caroline!"

"Over here!"

Her voice comes from behind me. Turning, I see her in the water nearby, clinging to the skiff. It didn't overturn after all.

"Are you all right?" Caroline yells. "Swim over to me!"

"I don't swim very well!" I shout back. It takes all my energy just to keep from sinking. I'm getting *so* tired . . .

❀ *Turn to page 178.*

W hen I return to my own time, I lie on the grass by the pond for a while. I need to think about my adventure and sort out my feelings. Finally I turn my back on the pond and take the path to my house.

When I reach the backyard, I see a blanket draped over the picnic table. I walk over and crouch down so that I can see inside. Britney and Sasha have dolls in there, and red plastic play dishes. I guess they're having a tea party in their fort. I think about Caroline and the *real* forts the military men are building in Sackets Harbor to protect the village from the British. I imagine my little sisters living in a time when forts weren't for play. The picture is so terrible that for a few seconds it's hard to breathe.

When I'm able to speak normally I ask, "Are you having fun in there?"

Both of them eye me warily, as if they're afraid that I might start yelling again. Sure enough, Britney says, "Are you still mad?"

"No," I assure them. "And if you want, I'll come back and play with you later."

Well, that cheers them right up. They love it when I spend time with them. And honestly, most of the time,

I love it too. I'm good at making up new make-believe games. Sasha loves to pretend, and Britney's so good at it that she could be on TV.

Spending time with them really isn't such a big deal, I think as I walk to the house. Suddenly a new idea pops into my head. My best friend was in the school play last year, and she wants to act in movies one day. I bet she'd be happy to help the twins do some little skit or song routine for Dad. I'd get to have fun with my friend *and* help keep Britney and Sasha too busy to miss Mom for a while.

I let myself in the back door. I don't see Mom, but Dad is slicing cheese at the counter. "Hi, Dad," I say quietly.

"Hello," he says. He puts the knife down and folds his arms, waiting.

"I'm sorry I yelled this morning," I tell him.

He smiles a little. "That's my girl." Fortunately, my dad never stays mad for long.

"Do you need some help?" I ask.

He steps away from the cutting board. "I'd appreciate that. I was starting to make macaroni and cheese for later, but I'll be late for work if I don't go get ready."

"Where's Mom?" I ask.

She's writing an e-mail to send to friends and family," he explains. "People are worried about her, and wondering if they can stay in touch when she's away at sea. She wants to reassure them."

I guess I've been thinking so much about my own worries that I haven't thought about the other people who are going to miss Mom after she goes to sea. I realize that making mac and cheese is what I can do to help a lot of people today.

I pick up the knife and get started. Dad gives my shoulder a squeeze. "Thanks."

"No problem," I say. "You can count on me."

≥ The End ≤

To read this story another way and see how different choices lead to a different ending, go back to page 67.
To read this story another way and see how different choices lead to a different ending, go back to page 67.

I 'd like to send a letter to my family," the man says. Then he grimaces at his bandaged hand. "But I burned myself badly the other day, and I'm not able to hold a pen. Might you be willing to—"

"Of course!" I assure him.

A few sheets of paper, a quill pen, and a little bottle of ink are sitting inside a small crate by his cot. I sit down on the floor. The boards are rough, but at least I'll have a flat surface to write on. I'm not sure how the pen works, so I dip the pointy end in the ink and touch it against the paper. A black blob of ink immediately makes a stain. "Oh, I'm sorry!"

He waves my worry aside. "I don't believe I've ever written a page without a blot," he tells me. "Now, here's how I'd like to begin."

He speaks slowly, giving me time to write. I make a whole lot more ink blots, but I do my best.

Dear Mary and children,
    I am sorry I felt compelled to leave without saying good-bye, but when I heard the militia was mustering, I knew I had to go.

OK, I know it's none of my business, but . . . this guy left home without even saying good-bye to his family? I put the pen down. Here I've been worried about how hard it will be to say good-bye to Mom. It would be a zillion times worse if she just disappeared without a word.

"Pardon me, sir," I say. "Did you really just take off? I mean—you left for war without telling your family where you were going?"

He looks away. "It was best."

It's hard not to frown at him. Men were pretty much in charge two hundred years ago, so maybe they figured they could just do whatever they wanted. "If you have a daughter," I say finally, "I imagine she would have really wanted to know that you were going."

His cheeks turn the reddish color of bricks. "Well, miss, I don't always find the right words when I'm in a conversation. Writing a letter lets me think through what truly needs saying."

"Oh." I nod slowly. Sometimes it *is* easiest to say what you mean in a letter. I pick up the pen, signaling that we can start again.

*I trust this finds you all well. Mary, I know
our neighbors will gladly help with the harvest.
You children must be obedient and helpful. Boys, if
you work hard, I will take you fishing when I return.
And my little Julia, I've found several pretty feathers
which I shall bring home for you. I know how you
love birds.*

That makes me smile. When he's finished dictating I say, "If you'd like, sir, I can mail this for you." I have no idea how letters get mailed in 1812, but Caroline will know. "And could you spare a sheet of paper so that I can write a letter of my own?"

⚙ *Turn to page 180.*

ou can do it," Caroline calls. "Don't you dare give up!"

My face is above water, but I know I can't last much longer. "Help me!" I yell. At least I try to yell. The words come out more like a croak. I can feel my heart thudding in my chest.

"Grab this!" Caroline wrestles one of the wooden oars free and sends it across the restless water. I manage to grab it and hold on tight. But when I try to lean on it, the oar goes under water.

"It won't keep you from sinking," Caroline calls. "Just hold on and steady yourself. Try to stop thrashing around."

That's not easy, but I'm exhausted. I let my arms go limp. To my surprise, just holding on to the solid oar does help me stay afloat. I lean on it gently and kick my legs. Slowly, I make my way to the skiff.

"Hold on to the boat," Caroline advises. "Papa taught me to never let go of the skiff. It won't sink."

Shivering, I clutch the edge of the skiff so tight that I may never be able to let go. It's full of water, but still afloat.

I look toward shore. "What do we do now?" I pant.

"Do you think someone will come rescue us?"

"No," Caroline says. "We'll have to rescue ourselves."

"R-rescue ourselves?" I repeat through chattering teeth. "How are w-we supposed to do that?"

❀ *Turn to page 182.*

O f course," the man tells me.

A burst of laughter rolls across the room, and I glance over my shoulder. Caroline must be telling a funny story. She's waving her hands as she talks, and several patients are grinning and leaning forward to hear. I bet that spending time with her will be the best thing that happens to them today.

And I pretty much know how they feel. I think for a moment, and then I lean over and start to write.

Dear Caroline,

I wanted to leave a letter for you to find after I'm gone. I'm so glad I had a chance to meet you, and I wish I could stay longer in Sackets Harbor. I can't, though.

I know you're worried about your father, and I can tell you're frustrated that you can't get him home. But you may not realize how much you truly are helping your family. You're helping win the war, too.

*This was a really, really, **really** special day. I have a lot of good memories. I also have a lot of new ideas about some things, so now I must go find my own family. Please don't ever forget me. I will never forget you.*

Since I never really got the hang of this feather pen, the page is spotted with ink, but Caroline will be able to read it. I sign my name and blow on the paper to dry the ink. Then I fold it away and tuck it into my pocket. I'll find a quiet time later to leave it for her.

⚙ *Turn to page 186.*

aroline's blonde hair is plastered to her face. Clinging to the skiff, she uses one hand to scrape a strand away from her eyes. "We're not too far from shore, see? If we hang on and kick, we'll soon be in shallow water."

I don't know if we can manage it, but since I don't have a better idea, I do what she says. It seems to take forever, but we inch our way toward shore.

Suddenly Caroline flashes me her special grin. "Look—I can stand up!"

My feet hit the bottom too. It feels mucky and unstable, but it is much, much, *much* better than being out in the lake. I feel hot tears in my eyes and suddenly I'm bawling like a baby.

For the first time, Caroline looks really frightened. "What's the matter?"

"I—I was just so *scared*!" I blubber. "I've always been scared of water."

"You *have*?" Now Caroline looks horrified. "Why didn't you say so before we got into the skiff?"

"It all happened really fast," I remind her, sniffling hard. "And—and I didn't want to be a big whiner."

Now Caroline looks confused. "A big whiner?"

For some reason, that's enough to make me stop crying. I pull myself together, because there's something I really need to say.

"I'm sorry, Caroline. It's my fault we ended up in the lake." I bite my lip. "If I hadn't stood up, it wouldn't have happened. Can you forgive me?" I would hate to go back to my own time knowing that Caroline blamed me for losing that British ship.

"You didn't know any better!" Caroline protests. "I should never have taken you out on the lake without making sure that you were comfortable in the skiff."

I let out a big whoosh of breath. "I guess we both could have made better choices today," I say, just like my dad always says when I do something dumb.

"I'm *glad* you were with me," Caroline adds. "The truth is, I stayed out longer than I should have. The wind was getting too strong. If I'd fallen into the lake all alone, I don't think I could have dragged the skiff to shore by myself. For somebody who is afraid of water, I think you've done quite well."

I actually begin to feel kind of proud of myself.

Just then a cold rain starts falling, like someone turned on a shower full-blast. Raindrops make little dimples in the lake's surface and stream down my face. "Oh!" I cry. "If only we had an umbrella!"

Caroline stares at me like I'm absolutely crazy. "We're already soaked," she points out. She starts to laugh, and *I* start to laugh, and we laugh so hard that my sides ache.

Finally, still giggling, we haul the skiff toward shore. It weighs a ton with all the water in it, but I know that together, we'll get the job done.

I should still be shivering, but I'm not. Helping lug the skiff warms me up on the outside. And knowing that I shoved right through my fear and helped save Caroline makes me feel toasty-warm on the inside, too. After all, I just faced one of my very worst fears—and survived! And not just survived, either—Caroline thought I did a really good job.

I'll take the memory of this adventure back home with me. It will remind me that when I have to, I can do more than I think I can—or more than I want to. I'll always worry about Mom, but now I feel confident that I can face saying good-bye to her, and survive the

long months to come. If I put my mind to it, I might even do quite well.

≥ *The End* ≥

To read this story another way and see how different choices lead to a different ending, go back to page 45.

he rainstorm hits Sackets Harbor when Caroline and I are halfway back to her house. We pull our wool shawls over our heads, but our shoes and the hems of our skirts are soaked and caked with mud by the time we race into the kitchen.

"Gracious, girls," Mrs. Livingston says. "Go straight upstairs and change out of those wet clothes. Leave your shoes down here so you don't track mud all over."

"You can borrow a dress of mine," Caroline tells me.

"And perhaps you'd both like to take a nap before supper," Mrs. Livingston suggests. "You've had quite a day."

She glances at me when she says that last bit. "Yes, ma'am," I say quickly, and follow Caroline out of the room.

Caroline leads me up a narrow flight of stairs to her bedroom. Once we've both peeled off our dirty stockings and hung our damp dresses on pegs, she finds me a nightgown to wear. Then she unfolds several spare blankets. "Since you're my guest, why don't you take my bed? I'll make a pallet on the floor," she says.

I don't know what "pallet" means, but I get the idea. Caroline has a beautiful four-poster bed, but it's

pretty narrow. She arranges the blankets on the floor, and I slip beneath her embroidered spread.

Soon her breathing gets deep and even, and I can tell that she's fallen asleep. I'm tired too, but I have so many thoughts buzzing around my head that I can't sleep. *Now is the time to slip away*, I realize sadly. I get up and silently put my dress back on. I won't be wearing it much longer, so the damp skirt won't be a problem. Fortunately I managed to keep my letter to Caroline dry. I unfold it and leave it on a little table beside the bed.

I creep down the stairs. I can hear Caroline's grandmother in the kitchen, so I head for the parlor, which should be empty. The room is full of all kinds of things I'd like to examine if I had more time—treasures made from seashells, model ships, a pretty embroidered screen-type thing near the fireplace. I'm not sure what it's used for, and it reminds me that there is lots more to learn about 1812.

Maybe you can come visit again sometime, I console myself. *But now, you need to go home.*

I get out the compass and let the dizziness come. When I open my eyes, I'm by the pond. I miss Caroline

already! But I'm also glad to be back home.

I walk to my house and see my parents and the twins in the backyard. "Are you feeling better?" Mom asks.

"Yes," I say.

"Play soccer with us!" Sasha cries, tugging on my sparkly T-shirt.

"I will soon," I promise. I realize I'm not quite ready to either talk to Mom or jump into a crazy soccer game with five-year-olds. "May I go inside for a bit first?" I ask my parents.

"Of course," Dad says. He looks at me thoughtfully, but he doesn't ask any questions.

Up in my bedroom, I grab a pen and the journal I kept for school last year and rip out one of the blank pages in the back.

Dear Mom,
I'm sorry I got so mad at you. I was just filled up with so many worries . . .

I scribble for a long time. It takes a whole page to tell her everything that makes me feel frightened or

sad about her going away. It feels *really* good to get everything down.

Then I end the letter this way: *All this doesn't mean that I'm not proud of you for joining the navy, because I am. And I always will be.*

After signing my name, I hide the letter in my desk drawer. When Mom leaves, I *will* go and see her off. I'll also tuck the letter in her things for her to find. I imagine her discovering it after her ship has left the dock, and the picture makes me smile.

Then I head back downstairs. Suddenly, a crazy game of family soccer sounds pretty good.

≥ *The End* ≤

To read this story another way and see how different choices lead to a different ending, go back to page 89.

ABOUT Caroline's Time

In 1812, when Caroline was nine, the United States had been an independent country for more than thirty years. But Great Britain had never respected America's independence. Over the years, the British navy captured more than 10,000 American sailors and forced them to serve on British ships. Britain blocked American ships from trading in foreign ports, devastating American businesses, and caused trouble for American settlers moving west. Finally, the U.S. had enough. It declared a second war against Britain.

By August 1812, when this story takes place, America and Britain had been at war for two months. Caroline's home of Sackets Harbor, New York, was no longer a quiet little village—it was the headquarters for the entire U.S. Navy on the Great Lakes. The British navy's headquarters were only thirty miles away, just across Lake Ontario in the colony of Upper Canada.

The American navy was working feverishly to erect forts, bring in troops, and build warships. British warships had already fired cannons at Caroline's village. A year later, a much bigger and bloodier battle would take place there.

As soldiers, sailors, marines, and army officers were called to duty, the war separated wives from their husbands and children from their fathers. Other men joined volunteer militia; when an attack seemed likely, signal guns rang out and riders raced on horseback through the countryside, alerting the militiamen to leave their homes and fight.

Some men, like Caroline's father, had no chance to fight. They were captured by the British and held on ships or in Canadian prisons for months or even years.

It was up to women and children to do the work that the men had left behind. Most women already worked very hard to keep their homes and families going. Women spun yarn and thread, wove cloth, sewed clothing, and made soap and candles. They grew and preserved food for their families. When war came, women had to keep their husbands' businesses going, too. Like Mrs. Abbott, who managed her husband's shipyard, many women ran their families' stores, inns, taverns, and farms. Women kept blacksmith forges blazing and printing presses running.

Some women didn't stop there. Women made daring trips into enemy territory to buy or beg for the release of their husbands or sons from prison. Other women rolled up their sleeves and joined in the fighting. Betsy Doyle was the wife of an American soldier who helped fire a cannon at Fort Niagara, New York. When her husband was captured during a fierce battle, she bravely took his place in the fighting. Enemy cannonballs fell all around her. Still she stood her ground, loading cannons until the battle ended.

By the time the war's last battle was fought in early 1815, America's men, women, and children had proved that they could protect their country's independence against the most powerful navy in the world.

Read more of CAROLINE'S stories,

available from booksellers and at *americangirl.com*

Classics

Caroline's classic series, now in two volumes:

Volume 1:
Captain of the Ship
When war breaks out and Papa is captured, Caroline must learn to steer a steady course without him.

Volume 2:
Facing the Enemy
The war comes closer and closer to Sackets Harbor. Can Caroline make the right decisions when the enemy attacks?

Journey in Time

Travel back in time—and spend a day with Caroline.

Catch the Wind
Go on a sail with Caroline, help her capture an enemy fort, or ride an American warship to a hidden bay! Choose your own path through this multiple-ending story.

Mysteries

More thrilling adventures with Caroline!

Traitor in the Shipyard
Caroline suspects one of Papa's trusted workers is an enemy spy.

The Traveler's Tricks
Caroline and Rhonda ride a stagecoach—right into trouble!

≥ A Sneak Peek at ≥

Captain of the Ship

A Caroline Classic

Volume 1

What happens to Caroline?
Find out in the first volume of her classic stories.

ncle John!" Oliver called sharply.

Papa scrambled to his feet.

"Has the wind picked up?" Caroline asked, although she could tell it had not—not very much, anyway. Then she heard a splash. It came from the Kingston side of the ship. She followed the others to the rail.

Three longboats were coming straight toward *White Gull*. Even from this distance, Caroline could see the British flag hanging limply over the boat. The men pulling on the oars wore blue and white uniforms. Each boat held about twenty men.

"Why are they working so hard to reach us?" Caroline asked.

Papa crossed his arms over his chest, frowning. "Something's wrong," he muttered. "I don't like this at all."

Caroline shoved the knotted line into her pocket with suddenly trembling fingers. "Papa?"

"You girls get below and stay there," he ordered.

Caroline and her cousin Lydia exchanged a wide-eyed look. Caroline's heart fluttered as she hurried down the steps to *White Gull*'s hold beneath the deck. There was a tiny galley for cooking, a couple of bunks,

and empty shelves where Oliver would store barrels of flour and potatoes and whatever else he might haul.

Lydia followed her below. "What do you think is wrong?"

"I can't imagine!" Caroline said. For a few moments the girls waited in uneasy silence. Then Caroline turned toward the steps.

"Caroline, stop!" Lydia hissed. "Your papa said—"

"I'm not going up on the deck," Caroline said in a low voice. She crept up the steps, crouching at the top so that she could listen.

"What's happening?" Lydia asked in a whisper.

"The British men are pulling closer," Caroline reported. "I can hear the little splashes from their oars."

A shout cut the afternoon: *"White Gull!* Strike your sails and prepare to be boarded!"

Caroline frowned. The British men were acting as if they owned all of Lake Ontario!

Papa's voice was forceful but calm. "What is your business with us?"

"Sir!" It was the same voice. "Prepare to be boarded at once, or we will open fire!"

Lydia gasped, and Caroline's mouth went dry.

Open *fire*? Why would the British men threaten to shoot? Papa and Oliver hadn't done anything wrong!

She peeked around the corner just as the *Gull*'s wood-and-rope ladder clattered against the ship's hull. A moment later, a tall hat popped above the rail. Then the man wearing that hat appeared, in a blue and white uniform coat with gold buttons. He swung one leg over the rail and jumped to the deck. Several sailors climbed on board after him.

"Explain yourself!" Papa demanded.

The British officer lifted his chin, looking haughty. "I am Lieutenant Morris. I—"

"We are an unarmed ship from Sackets Harbor," Oliver interrupted. "We're not carrying cargo."

Go away, Caroline ordered the British man silently. *Just go away!*

Papa planted his feet a little more firmly on the deck. "You have no right to threaten this vessel."

The British officer let one hand rest on the hilt of the long sword hanging by his side. "I have *every* right, sir," he snapped. "Perhaps you have not yet received the news."

"What news?" Papa's tone was hard. Caroline

could tell that he was very angry.

The British officer gave him a small, cold smile. "Why, of war, sir."

War? Caroline's stomach clenched. She heard Lydia gasp.

Lieutenant Morris paced a few steps, studying the sloop. "Your American president has declared war on Great Britain," he continued. "I am seizing this vessel in the name of His Majesty King George the Third. You are now my prisoners."

No! Caroline wanted to scream. *No, no, no!* But the words felt frozen inside.

"My father is a British citizen who lives in Upper Canada!" Oliver cried. "You have no cause to seize this ship."

"This ship is flying an American flag," said Lieutenant Morris. "My duty is clear."

Oliver launched himself forward with an angry snarl. Caroline's heart seemed to leap into her throat as the British sailors reached for their weapons.

Papa managed to grab Oliver. "Think of the girls," Papa muttered.

Oliver instantly went still.

"We have two young ladies aboard," Papa told Lieutenant Morris. "I trust that my daughter will be safely returned to her mother in Sackets Harbor. At *once*. And—"

"Papa, no!" Caroline cried. All the men's heads turned as she scrambled into the open.

"Caroline, be still," Papa said in a voice so stern that she swallowed her protests.

Then Papa turned back to the British officer. "And my young niece lives not three miles from here. Will you make provisions for the girls?"

"Why—why, of course." Lieutenant Morris's voice had lost its mocking tone. "Your niece will be given safe haven in Kingston until her parents can fetch her. I will escort your daughter back to Sackets Harbor myself, under a flag of truce. I give you my word."

Papa left the knot of men and crouched in front of Caroline. "I know what's best, daughter," he said, taking her hands in his.

"I don't want to go with them," Caroline whispered.

"I know," he said gently. "But you must obey me, and be brave."

Caroline stared at Papa through tears. She didn't

feel brave at all. Lydia had come on deck behind her, and she stood clinging to her brother. Lydia looked as if she wasn't feeling brave, either.

"Remember, you are a sailor's daughter," Papa told Caroline. "Everyone must sometimes face stormy seas. Good sailors learn to ride the storms through to better weather. Can you do that?"

"I—I'll try."

"Stay steady, Caroline. Obey your mama. Give her and your grandmother whatever help they need while I'm away." Papa's voice was urgent. "I must have your *promise.*"

Caroline swiped at her eyes with one hand. "I promise, Papa."

"Make me proud." Papa squeezed her hands before rising. He looked at the lieutenant. "Let's get on with it."

As Lieutenant Morris snapped some orders to his men, Lydia gave Caroline a fierce hug. "Good-bye," she whispered in Caroline's ear.

"Good-bye," Caroline echoed. She felt numb inside. When would she see Lydia again? When would she see *any* of them again?